OFFSPRING

OFFSPRING

A NOVEL

▼

Jonathan Strong

ZOLAND BOOKS

Cambridge, Massachusetts

First edition published in 1995 by
Zoland Books, Inc.
384 Huron Avenue
Cambridge, Massachusetts 02138

PUBLISHER'S NOTE

This work was supported by a grant from the National Endowment
for the Arts.

The first chapter appeared in *Hanging Loose*.

Book design by Boskydell Studio
Printed in the United States of America

10 9 8 7 6 5 4 3 2 1

This book is printed on acid-free paper, and its binding materials have
been chosen for strength and durability.

Library of Congress Cataloging-in-Publication Data
Strong, Jonathan.
Offspring : a novel / by Jonathan Strong — 1st ed.
p. cm.
ISBN 0-944072-55-0
1. Parent and child — Illinois — Chicago Region — Fiction.
2. Suburban life — Illinois — Chicago Region — Fiction. 3. Boys —
Illinois — Chicago Region — Fiction. 4. Chicago Region (ill.) —
Fiction. I. Title.
PS3569.T698O37 1995

813'.54 — dc20   94-35508
CIP

for FRANK WALLACE

And he shall turn the heart of the fathers to the children, and the heart of the children to their fathers, lest I come and smite the earth with a curse.

MALACHI 4:6

PART ONE

▼   ▼   ▼

1

BUT IF THE world was different, it wouldn't seem so odd the way we live.

Pick up my goblet by the green stem and watch how the silvery wine looks green in the lamplight. A sip. Another thought.

How our three boys have fewer points of reference. It's hard for us to plot where they are. We keep them in the margins, on a scale of their own. For them, home life can only be meant as we have it. And everyone else lives in some other hemisphere, which doesn't interest them much.

The dog is suddenly here, a nose on my knee.

And darkness falls. Hear them scraping beneath the basement, shoveling and scooping, pulling up another load for the wheelbarrow. "Are you tired of watching them, Spode?"

Another sip. I have unwound. The furry head watches, tilting and puzzled. "We already had our walk," I tell him. "How long is your memory?"

All the light in the room is glowing from his eyes and

from the greenish wine and the green glass lampshade. We feel surrounded in darkness.

"You want Izzy, don't you! You're never at ease until everyone's at home. What can we do but wait? Down there the boys will be quitting soon. I'll make them shower so you can lick off their legs."

Lean back, sip. Ignore that paw. Another thought. How our three boys prefer the company of each other. Their schoolmates haven't learned the words they know, wouldn't care for the games they play. But no one gives our boys trouble. They're strong from their digging, and good-looking, so they're tolerated.

It was something Obadiah saw on television when he was small, a man with yellow teeth growing slantwise through the skin of his cheeks. That's all we could worm out of him. And then several years of talk about wanting a tunnel. When his brothers were old enough to be of help, they all set to work.

Spode goes to watch at the window and catch the headlights turning onto Greenwood. Even if she's late, it won't dishearten him. He knows what must come next.

I hear footsteps.

"Did you latch the cellar door?"

"But we didn't dump the last load. It's raining," says Obadiah somewhere behind me.

"Is it?"

I haven't heard or seen rain. There was a soft gray sky when I got off my bus. Everything will be shiny when Izzy comes, her headlights on the shiny street and the dead shiny leaves.

"We're going to shower, Poppa."

So I didn't need to make them do it. On their own they want to do it. Obadiah's whistle, but Spode won't be budged from the window now. My wine seems suddenly all the more warming. I can hear faint rain on the window behind the couch.

Laughter upstairs as their clothes pull inside out and wad up in piles on the floor. A last drop is circling the bottom of my goblet. Shower water starts to gurgle down the pipe by the kitchen door. Spode knows that sleek sound of a passing car is not Izzy's. He understands signals I don't.

The last drop.

I'm up.

▼ ▼ ▼

Malachi has something to say to his mother, who would rather not be spoken to right now.

"They ask me funny questions at school. Because of the scratches on my hands."

Izzy is polishing up an old brass door knocker so it will sell better.

"Not my teacher," Malachi goes on, "but this lady who comes around. Mrs. Schnell."

"Let me see your hands," I say and it's true they are scratchier than usual.

"Because we hit a gravelly part this week, sharp edges," says Malachi.

"Have any gardener's gloves at the shop, Iz?"

"That's a thought."

"But how did you answer the lady's questions?" I ask, imagining Mrs. Schnell's vision of our neglectfulness.

"Me and my brothers fight a lot, I told her."

I wonder if Malachi wishes that were so.

Izzy sets the door knocker on the counter. It does shine now. I've finished the dishes and shake out the dish towel like a flag. Spode expects a game.

"Can I have some glue, Momma?"

Izzy finds it for him in a different drawer from the one I'd have tried first. Then what is in that other one? I'm not going to look, I'm going to puzzle over it. Why wouldn't the glue be in with the string? There's string in that other drawer, and tape — duct tape, electrical tape, brown paper tape for packages. I'm sure there are the extra keys and some rolls of putty for the windows.

"Your dog wants to go out, Malachi." She has to keep reminding him he's theirs. And then Malachi slips out too without a coat.

"Isabel."

"Isn't this a handsome thing?"

"So let's keep it for ourselves," I say.

"But why have a knocker when we have knuckles?"

"Beautiful knuckles," I say, looking at hers.

"Stiffening, stiffening."

To show me, she stretches out ten slender fingers in front of my eyes. Never a ring on them. I kiss a palm, then another, then the first again and hold it, press it to my cheek, then to my other cheek. Her neck is bending down. From above I see all of her brown hair. We take a slow dance step by ourselves.

But Malachi comes in with a handful of wet twigs and the tube of glue in his shirt pocket. Mist from the green plaid flannel evaporates in our warm kitchen.

"And where's your friend?"

"He didn't want to come back in, Momma."

Spode may wait hours for Izzy to come home, but once she's in the door he doesn't take much notice. When she calls out back now, he won't even come.

I drift toward the living room, passing our shadowy bathroom, our bedroom door. I hear nothing at the foot of the stairs but their quiet voices planning something up there.

My perfect chair. All those chairs that came through Izzy's shop before this ideal one. She knew it would be, lugged it home full of expectation. The chair looked splayed and humped to me. But when you've sat in it, she said, then! She knows me. It hits my back exactly right. Now the dark blue nubbles are wearing off, especially where Spode puts his chin, alone in the house.

I could pick up an old atlas to leaf through, but why not just wait for Izzy to come in and sit, and look, and talk? Did she take it in about the scratches on Malachi's hands? And the others have their marks too. Their knees are worse than boys their age are supposed to have. They never took my suggestion of kneepads.

"Coffee, Linc?" sails in from the kitchen.

Her usual question and my answer, "Yes please," as usual.

A worry. That our boys are going to live in the world longer than we are. That we may be keeping them from something. We're careful not to blame each other, but we do sometimes blame ourselves together. There's something behind us, Lincoln, Izzy has said, a kind of secret pact we've made. We have our own tyrannies.

She comes in, tray and all.

"Aha, a new touch."

"It came into the shop. Might as well use it once first."

There seem to be more trays than anything else. Most have designs you might not believe anyone would care to look at, but this one is black with flowers, in their own right colors, twining out from under our blue coffeepot.

"I think I'll make more use of trays, door knockers, things of that sort. You've set me thinking, Linc."

That is always a danger. Izzy's new ideas take hold in minutes. Malachi is like her. His need for twigs came to him only after she reminded him the dog had to go out.

"But I'm bringing home a different knocker. Iron, not so imposing. Should we hold on to this tray?"

"And what other things of that sort?" I ask.

"Napkin rings? Trivets? I don't know yet."

She takes her corner of the couch and sets the tray on the coffee table where it belongs. A rattling of spoons. A sugar spoon and one for each cup, souvenir spoons from other people's travels long ago, not matching, where a single spoon would do.

"All the more dishes to wash."

"But to slow us down, Linc. Like our boys' full names."

She has her point. It's been our natural direction all along.

▼   ▼   ▼

I'm tucking Zephaniah into bed before the other two are ready for sleep. A light glows from the seams of Malachi's quilt. He's under there reading, like in a tent, he told me. A lopsided bird's nest, I think it's meant to be, and the tube of glue on the floor by his bed. And Obadiah's around the corner at his desk, the gooseneck lamp bent low over his plans so as not to keep his brothers awake.

"Sleepy," says Zephaniah, struggling against it.

"A quick one then."

He nods and nuzzles his forehead at my knee. I change my voice and begin the new story:

"Spode had a lot to accomplish. The last of his people, the big gruff one with the tummy, was off to catch his morning bus. The latch had been firmly twisted behind him, the key removed, and his steps had become fainter until even the sensitive Spode couldn't make them out. In fact, the delicate aura that told him one of his people was in range had dissipated entirely. A silent house at last, but no time to settle into his favorite nubbly blue chair and give his chin a rest, no time to nose into a cupboard for an extra nibble. Spode had to get on with things. His three smaller people, the ones who spent so much time excavating, had no idea that even as they dug, so dug Spode. And to conceal his operation he had his own private door, a tea tray bearing the likeness of a cocker spaniel, done in inlaid pennies with dime eyes and a nickel nose. He had dragged it from a lower shelf in the kitchen, bumped it down the basement stairs and nudged it up into the crawl space under the front porch. No one had missed it. Now, sliding it aside on this particular morning, he revealed a sight familiar to his own eyes but unknown to the rest of the household: a dusty black tunnel, curving down and around and up again to emerge outside under the porch stairs where he had his hatch, a dented-up garbage can lid, to keep out cats."

"I saw that old lid under there," says a quiet voice.

"Don't ever move it, Zephaniah. We don't want Spode knowing we've caught on."

"Well, go on, Poppa."

"And so he was out. He could stroll by Iola's house and serenade at her window. He could go the other way and see if Scoper could get his late-sleeping master to let him out for a romp. But Spode had something else in mind. His furry brown paws took him across Greenwood and through a yard, under a bush, down a driveway, and thus block by block across the village till he'd made his way to what he thought of as the edge of things. The last street ended in a turnaround, and beyond the last house began woods, which went all the way to a little meadow, which sloped down to bulrushes and cattails by a muddy lagoon."

"We took Spode there once."

"That's how he knew to go there. That's why he always goes back."

"But what does he do there all by himself?"

"Perhaps we'll save that for tomorrow night."

"He's building a house for himself," says Zephaniah.

"Then you think up the sort of house he might be building. Think about it till you fall asleep."

Malachi is flashing his light on and off, a signal to give him his good-night kiss too. I lift a flap of his quilt, lean in. It smells of sweaty pajamas.

Around the corner, Obadiah is bending over his plans. Unnoticed, I kiss the soft hair at his neck on my way out.

▼　▼　▼

We are in bed where everything is still. It's our island, green above the blue carpet. We touch and don't touch each other here in all different ways. She's been going over her ledger, lower lip between thumb and forefinger, rubbed, pulled at. Now she picks up the next in her pile of fat old books, slightly moldy, probably from someone's dead great-aunt's shelves. "Twilight Sleep by Edith Wharton," she informs me. Already on page one she's chuckling over it. But I won't ask her why. She has her reading. It's the old histories and travel books and nature studies that come into the shop she passes on to me. This particular heavy geography I'm staring at now, The Ocean Floor.

The hillocks of our green island where there are our knees or toes, the mountains my stomach, her breast. One window open to hear the night rain. Not a sound from Obadiah's corner above us. We expect his desk chair to scrape the floor occasionally. And he keeps getting up from bed in the night when he has a further idea to write down before it leaves him. He's our ponderer.

These evenings keep hovering around us, longer than by day I dared hope they would seem. Because of winter coming and everything drawing inside. To be able to sleep under our green quilt again and hear the purr of the furnace coming on once in the night. Spode sleeps now by the vent in the living room. He hears the rush of flame down there, then the fan coming on, then miraculous warm air ruffles his fur.

I can imagine the map of our house like some Pacific Ocean with warm air currents circling furniture islands over carpet seas. And now it's the doldrums that have idled me so.

"How are you doing?" Izzy asks me, shutting her book.

"Quiet."

"Nothing stirring?"

I think it over while she orders her tabletop, Wharton on top of The Prodigal Parents by Sinclair Lewis, which will come next. Why buy the latest books when so many old ones keep turning up? Their thick pages, their wide margins, the good feel of them. Izzy shuts off her light then settles in beside me, quilt to our chins.

Instead of answering, I ask, "How about you?"

"Lost, sometimes, a little lost. Everything passing through, coming and going. The old people coming in the shop, nothing quite right with anything. Not much of a take on a given day, worrying if it will add up. There I am in my car and you on your bus, going our separate ways. The children at school, our house sitting here warming and cooling, warming and cooling through the day without us."

She reaches around me. Now I reach around her. She listens at my chest.

"Something is stirring," she says.

It's the coffee that makes us think faster when our bodies only grow tired. And then later it weaves into our dreams.

"You mustn't be lost. I'll track you down and find you, Iz, wherever you are."

"Fill me with some of your quiet," she says.

And I imagine we will begin a kind of lovemaking we do sometimes where we hardly move, where we live suspended and our thoughts will go somewhere we haven't imagined but our bodies will stay almost still.

▼ ▼ ▼

I wake from dreams. Something cold. I was in Persia where winds tear across deserts. And whatever is happening in the world now was long past. The face in Obadiah's memory was haunting me, fearsome yellow teeth through the skin of a cheek. I could switch on my light and wake Izzy. She's breathing softly, lying on her right side, turned away from me, lumpy like a range of hills in moonlight. So the sky has cleared. There's bright moonlight on the rim of the white bowl on her dresser. I'll have to get up and put something over it if I'm to fall back to sleep.

Lost the dream now. Long travels, I think, alone, and a yellow face, a ragged cheek. Awaiting or pursuing? No sense of direction.

Now then, instead, my terrible game, to fall back to sleep. It can be happy or sad.

I look into our future. So this is what has happened. Our boys are grown. They will have nothing to do with us anymore. Obadiah has never made a friend. He only works. He sits at a desk in some high building working on something no one else can understand. Malachi is long gone, west, east, we have no idea. Not a call, never a letter. He took nothing with him. Zephaniah lives with us, of course. It suits him, for now. But we never see him. The door slams late at night, he stomps up the stairs. He's installed a door at the top, with a lock. He's supposed to pay us rent. He sleeps until we're off to work. What he does during the day we have no idea. Disappears on weekends. Back when Spode died, that was the end of Zephaniah's life with the family. We don't know what our boys look like anymore. Taller than I, silent, shadows. Do they still talk with each other? Do they know where each of them is, stay in secret touch? And our own parents still tell us over and over how they knew this would happen. What did we expect from the odd way we lived? Sometimes I go crawl around in the old tunnels under our house and try to remember when our boys were small.

No, but I'm not asleep yet. That didn't do it.

▼   ▼   ▼

A long night. In and out of a kind of half sleep. The bowl's shiny rim faded, the bottom of the window shade flapped when a breeze stirred. I spent coherent moments imagining maps, maps to be ordered, maps to be sent out, misplaced maps I wished I might come across again, buried in piles in corners. And that world map that got me started, hanging over my bed all my childhood with names of places no longer to be found, the Anglo-Egyptian Sudan, Palestine, Persia. I didn't know the world would change, didn't know it already had. That map gradually gave way at its folds, Mother replaced it, an up-to-date one in paler colors. She thought I'd be pleased.

Enough.

Perhaps it's light enough to attend to Spode. He'll be grateful for the early company. So I slip out of bed, bend around and into my bathrobe. Izzy is purring through her last dreams.

Spode raises his chin, never quite sure he recognizes me at this hour. Here I am in the world again, he's thinking. Oh yes, that wall, this chair, that person in the doorway, familiar smell. And there's something I have to do outside, can't remember, I'll know when I get there. Stretch.

Then he pads after me to the kitchen and waits at the door. His little brain functions more speedily. Out he goes, nosing around the boys' latest dumpings till he finds the right slope to lift his leg against. There is a slight mist rising. Behind it, the row of houses under their low-pitched roofs, their pastels not quite differentiated this early. The next house on this side sits empty still, windows shadeless, unsalable. Back behind, beneath her yellow back porch light, diffused in this mist, the old widow is letting out the skittery white poodle Spode doesn't consider a dog. Spode sniffs his way across our clumpy grass ignoring the insistent yips. I follow him through the window over the sink, then through the dining room windows, with my blinky eyes.

Next door on this side, the youngest Etherege kid wheels her bike out from their garage, which is becoming beige, heaves herself onto the seat and coasts overweightedly down their driveway. She swerves to avoid Spode, who charges out from the bushes, and weaves casually off up the street to collect her load of Friday papers.

I'm somehow at the front window, staring into our shadowy porch, out through its blackened screens and across Greenwood. Shades snap in the pale bluish house on the corner. I catch sight of shapes rushing about inside. These movements, these changes of color — Izzy never sees them.

Spode tears back into our yard. I'll have to make it to the back door before he scratches. Dashing, my ankle tangles on the splayed-out right front leg of my chair. Down the hall of darkened doors, and I make it. Open. But no Spode. The widow's house is growing limier in the drier light, her porch light is sharper-edged dull yellow. There's Spode sniffing the further mounds. Our backyard is like a moon, little rubble mountains and craters. Izzy has ambitions for it next spring.

Soft padding feet above me. It's Malachi. He's always too edgy to sleep late.

▼   ▼   ▼

"Momma, I want my usual bowl," Zephaniah complains.

"Well get it then."

But he doesn't know where it is. Last seen holding three forgotten raisins and tucked under one end of the couch, but I'm not going to tell him.

"But I have to eat," he says.

"What's wrong with the bowl you have?" Obadiah asks.

Zephaniah holds up the last of a set that came through Izzy's shop back when she first started and points at discolored lumps around the rim, meant to represent raspberries.

"He thinks those are warts," says Malachi.

Zephaniah gives us a smug look, imagining we acknowledge the justice of his complaint.

Izzy leans over him, coffeepot held out behind her for balance, and switches the warty bowl for Obadiah's smooth brown-striped lunch-counter sort of bowl. Then I ladle out his oatmeal and pass on to patient Obadiah, then to fidgeting Malachi. Our overworked toaster, big and quirky, rounded like a silver bosom, begins to hum and three brown slices ascend. My first sip of Izzy's good coffee.

Spode senses cheerful company in the dining room. Every morning he patters in, after his upstairs inspection of interesting bed smells. Our breakfast, another marker of his long day.

The sun rises above the Etherege garage and hits me in the eyes. I can't see my family down the table. Wait a few minutes till the brightness slips up behind the window shade. By then I'll have set down an empty coffee cup on my mat, Izzy will be dressing and the boys still arguing jelly, jam and marmalade preferences with methodical thoroughness.

▼ ▼ ▼

They are gone. The fainter and fainter whir of Izzy's tires on Greenwood, then on Jackson.

Thoughts may also leap backwards. My other terrible game of what if we hadn't or what if I hadn't. But I mustn't.

Stack the bowls, jangle the spoons and knives into the top juice glass, the jars with their annoyingly uninterchangeable lids again properly arrayed on the lazy Susan, the crumbs swept into the warty bowl. Balance it all to the kitchen. Run the hot. Spode goes to check his own bowl for a last film of food. He knows it isn't the weekend quite yet. Loneliness awaits him.

But if I hadn't ever?

Back in my old childhood room under my map, the old map, the first map. There it was, every place I could possibly go. And Isabella in her old room too, perched above the lakeshore, hearing the purl of waves. We hardly knew each other, seen down rows in school assemblies, across playing fields. Stiff new blue jean legs encased my pink softness. Like Obadiah, on some verge, three times his age ago.

Our five juice glasses sparkling in the rack, the last washed still steaming.

Still. If I had never left the old room, now the odd bachelor, the never grown. But I'd be busy with collections, catalogs. Only no one else to look at them. They'd stretch back in tipping piles into the crawl spaces under the eaves.

We don't know what he does up there, Mother would always have to be explaining. We don't ask. We gave up on Lincoln ages ago. He comes down for his meals. Occasionally he'll step outside.

But our Doug and Gale have turned out all right — two out of three's not so bad, Father would put in, to unembarrass her.

And already the glasses, the bowls are dry. How long do I daydream? It takes an instant to imagine my possible lives.

And if I were to stay home today?

No, I mustn't. Outside it has all begun again.

NOW, AFTER COFFEE, Douglas has decided to be quiet. I
pretend to dip into Mother's latest mystery, carefully marking her place, but catch him staring out the bay window
at rain. This morning before we came, Izzy said to remember my brother has only his Sarie now, and only half the
time, and he doesn't know what to do with her without
her mother. So I did remember and I'm remembering again.
I look at him now. He's almost alone. There he sits, droplets
spattering the panes beyond. He droops, the robustness at
dinner gone out of him.

Oh come off it! was what he said at the table. Now Doug,
said Mother. But it wears me out, Linc's refusal, he said.
Dougie, what business is it of yours? I tried to say in my
calmest voice. It's my business, he said, it's family business, and he faced us square-shouldered, braced, from
across the table. It isn't your business, Izzy said gently in
our defense. And then Mother said that everything was
everybody's business, but not this way, children!

Then Father changed the subject from his end, empty
chair beside him where Lauren always used to sit. He asked

where our boys had disappeared to. True, Sarie had taken them upstairs to watch the television, but since television doesn't interest them, I was sure they were already off in the attic, crawling around dirtying their knees. It's what they look forward to, visiting here, I said, thinking: Our boys, who always play together, who won't play with anyone else, and not with their cousin Sarie.

So what is this I'm pretending to read? A green-clad man in a duck blind. Hunting Season, by one of Mother's regular purveyors. I used to find her reading in bed, a leafy green dust jacket slipped an inch up a purple spine. Now she gets them in paperback. Hours a day with them, hours to pass now we have grown.

Douglas and I. Galena and I, and Douglas. Galena and Douglas. The spaces between us.

We had our own boys one right after the other supposing it was simpler. Obadiah took it as the yearly event, expected yet another brother when he turned three. We said he'd have to be content with two. Then could we have a sister? he wondered. Oh your mother's too tired, Izzy said. Someday, perhaps, you boys will supply each other with sisters-in-law, how about that? But the prospect of marrying anyone but Izzy didn't attract Obadiah at three.

And if we'd had a daughter?

Sarie, too alone now with Doug, every other weekend. She dresses like she was seventeen. He takes her to a movie, out to dinner. He's trying to be steady with her. Look at his steadiness, how solidly he sits, how immovable the slump, the dead weight, staring. He should go watch television with her, not stare at rain.

Snap shut this cracked-spined book. I have to move about.

▼   ▼   ▼

But Sarie isn't in the television room. There's her angora sweater scrunched white in the corner of the red corduroy couch. On the end table, her pale pink lipstick peeks out from its gold case like the rarely seen penis of Spode. She hasn't turned the picture off, just the sound.

So what do I hear? They can be like scrabbling squirrels. But then a wicked laughter coming through the ceiling. Sarie's? I could go up and terrify them. I could slip off my boots, pad up those narrow stairs, listen for whereabouts, go in through the cupboard in my old room, sneak, sneak along the crawl space. And there they might be, under an eave with a flashlight — it's possible — Sarie's blouse open, letting them touch her breasts.

But I can't decide. No, from the window seat at the next stair landing I'll watch the rain like my brother. And thinking what falls out there on our parents' front yard trickles half a mile east into Lake Michigan and through lake to lake to the ocean and what falls around back seeps into swamps and streams to river and other rivers, finally to the gulf. This slight ridge, this subsidiary continental divide, unmarked, unnoticed except maybe by one map-crazed boy. How back then I knew I was in fact significantly placed. I'd watch from this soft-padded window seat how the rain fell on gentle slopes of grass. And Isabel then, right above the very lakeshore itself in another sort of house — modern house we called it — plate glass, cement, none of these creakings or rattlings. Our childhood nests.

And now we live, smaller, eleven miles to the west and south, a bungalow in the seepage.

Her steps coming up to me.

"It's quiet down there, Linc."

"Should I go liven them up?"

"You don't have to," she says, nearing.

"Squeeze in here then."

It's a tight fit between my knees. Her head stretches back, cool forehead to my cheek.

"He's very unhappy," she says, meaning Doug.

"But at dinner he told us we're doing things dangerously wrong. His word was 'dangerous,' wasn't it? When he's more dangerous than we are!"

"Who's to say what danger is?" says Izzy, nuzzling further in.

"But why always drag it out, why does he, why keep dragging it out?"

We both know some standard psychological reasons. But I want a new kind of reason, I think, a reason to do with demons: that my brother is possessed by a demon. I can't tell Izzy that. She would like to fall asleep between my knees, have rainy Sunday afternoon linger awhile, forget boys upstairs, family downstairs, forget shop tomorrow, house, everything.

"Where's Sarie?" she asks.

"Oh, in the attic with them."

"We should call them down. Your mother expects her game now."

"And Sarie?"

"Let's talk to her, Linc. Let's take her out walking."

▼   ▼   ▼

"But my boyfriend's down there and I've got a room all set up with my stuff and that's where I go to school now and have my friends so when I come back up here there's nothing to do and I have to just sit and talk to my dad. He doesn't have cable. That bedroom's still like when I was a little girl."

She's talking. She has plenty to say, so we don't stop her.

"I'd rather be with my boyfriend. His name's Darrell Quong. He's Chinese-American. He has short bristly black hair that stands up. It looks really great. You'd like him. He's a bit short for me. That's all right, I don't mind."

All the big oaks, and the elms saved from disease, hang heavy with rain, leaves yellowing, ready to let go. The humpbacked old street, shiny, black, without a car, without a person, no one even visible in windows. Houses are taller here and far apart. We would have brought Spode, but Mother doesn't want him coming in with wet paws. Now he could be running ahead of us, across a wide lawn: Sniff, sniff, hmmm, I've been here before. He'd run free in frantic investigation.

Izzy's hands in the pockets of her wet army jacket, her head bending forward, wetness all over her hair. She's holding herself tight to keep warm. And Sarie's arms float free in her dad's orange slicker. She tosses her head in the rain, talking and talking. So Izzy asks her, "What do you make of your cousins?"

"Obadiah got taller."

"It's beginning, it won't be long," I say.

"His feet are huge! He's going to be tall like you, Unc Linc."

"What do you make of him, as a character I mean?" Izzy asks.

"They're all still little kids. Darrell can never remember their long names when I talk about them. I told him about their tunnel. He thinks they sound weird. What are they doing, digging to China? he says. But it's just their hobby, sort of, what they like doing, I tell him. He knows I like them better than my other little cousins. He knows how I can't stand Aunt Gale. He knows how she can't stand my mom. He thinks it's terrible what we went through from her."

"I'd like to meet this Darrell Quong," says Izzy, since he's all Sarie wants to talk about.

"What about Malachi?" I ask.

"What about Malachi?"

"And what do you make of him?"

"Oh, Malachi, well, he told me how this teacher is out to get him. He's sure she's out to get him. She's always asking him these questions. She's always stopping him in the hall. He says she looks him in the eye and he starts shaking."

My boots have darkened in the rain. The cold wet reaches into my numbing toes. But I feel dinner in my stomach heating me up, blueberry pie dispersing through me and the coffee agitating my bowels.

▼   ▼   ▼

"Malachi came up with QUAGGA on a triple!" Mother is still stunned. "I had to go look it up," she's telling me. "An extinct wild ass, Lincoln!"

"He reads animal books under his covers at night."

"I know, I know. Last time it was ZEBU. I should expect it from him."

"Zebu's not extinct," I hear Malachi say.

The boys are lying on the braided rug behind the couch, rearranging the letter tiles. Their object, after the game, is to achieve a more satisfyingly clever outcome, as if tiles had been drawn exactly when they were most required. No one wins now. It's their cooperative puzzling out.

"We can take the LOV off the E and put it in front of CANOES," says Obadiah.

"LOVCANOES?" says Zephaniah, who gets a brotherly punch on his shoulder for not seeing what Obadiah means.

As usual, now, Father has gone to lie down. "Doug's up with the television, finally having quit fussing," Mother says. Apparently he's been anxious to get going. He didn't realize we were taking Sarie out walking, so I must go apologize. "The remarkable things that come through your shop!" I hear Mother saying as I climb the stairs. Izzy has resorted to inventory stories.

Sarie has put her sweater on and pulled the sleeves up tight on her pale arms. She stares at the screen too, and they don't look over at me. The thing is to sit on the arm of the couch and pretend to watch with them.

"Is it about over?"

"Just started," says Doug.

"I've seen this one, Dad."

"So see it again."

"It's a good one though," she says.

"Linc, you took me to this one, back before I was old enough to go to drive-ins."

It's coming back to me. A protoplasmal glob like mint jelly will soon slime its way out of that old lady's fish tank.

"What I admire about these movies is how totally dumb

they are," says Sarie. "Kids must've been dumber in your day."

"We're still dumber," says Doug.

I'm a little shaky. I do remember that green glob. It will slip along that windowsill with those filmy curtains blowing.

"Come on," says Doug, "get the boys to come watch. We'll all watch. Izzy will watch. Even Mother will watch, if we can stop her from asking stupid questions. We can wake Father up and he'll watch. It's a family thing, Lincoln. Call the boys. It's a Sunday treat. They've had their game with Mother. We can all relax."

"Sssh," says Sarie, "I'm listening."

"They wouldn't want to," I say, growing queasy.

"Goddammit, they would!"

"They don't watch television, Doug. They never turn it on."

"Goddammit! A harmless movie like this! You could make them watch it. Force them to, till they get to like it. Oh to hell with it!"

He gets up, knocking Sarie with his clumsy knees, slams his fist at the set so it shuts off.

"Dad!"

"I can't stand it. I've had it. It makes me sick. We're going. I'm taking you to the movies. What movie do you want to see, Sarie? I'll take you to any movie you want within ten miles."

▼　▼　▼

Mother has poured herself a very little brandy, and the three of us are to settle into the opposing love seats by the fire.

"Mother, I'll tell you what it is. He's possessed by a demon."

Izzy presses her calf against mine, a sign of our attachment through unsettled moments, and we both look up, across at her, with her snifter, her bony-knuckled fingers divided two and two around the stem, her thumb rubbing the bowl. Pensive Mother on Sunday afternoon, my brother's mother too. She's not going to give us a smile. But she saw him! He just grabbed Sarie's arm and pulled her out the front door without a word.

"Well, it's my simple theory anyway," I say.

"You're being subversive, Lincoln." Sip.

"Eldest children are always the more subversive," I say.

"Do tell!" Her eyebrows humorously raised. Sip.

"Well come on, Mother, it's either a demon or it's an awfully prolonged adolescence."

"And you won't let Doug have what he wants," she says. "You've entrenched your battle long since. It's only more of the same."

A swirl, a sniff, no sip. Doug has her perpetual sympathy.

I sense Izzy's elbow hovering on the love seat near mine. "Our boys seldom even skirmish," she says, without managing to capture Mother's attention. So now Izzy will be silent.

"But Doug claims we're doing things dangerously wrong," I say because I can't keep off it. "Who's he!"

"Yes, we parents often are dangerous, aren't we," says Mother. "Ever notice? It's a premise of family life."

I don't answer. She's switched it to herself of course. Did I once say she was dangerous?

"But children can accommodate," she says. "It's that you've always been unaccommodating, Lincoln — your absolute side, your world of your own. Doug only wants to engage in your secrets, that's all."

Father's on the stairs. He's had his nap and didn't catch any of the set-to. Mother won't make anything of it to him because it's nothing he hasn't already been hearing, for decades.

"Where have the boys disappeared to now?" he asks before he's all the way down.

Mother waits to answer, knowing he won't hear her yet.

It's Isabel who says, "They're out in the rain — don't worry, they won't come in again with their muddy feet." It's more for Mother's ears.

"Now don't tell me, Mother, you would've sat eagerly watching that mutating glob for two hours, commercials and all," I say. In my own adolescent sulk now.

"I heard Douglas drive off," Father says out there to the creaking staircase. We wait for him. Darkening fast in all the windows. Izzy, faithful, always with me.

"I've been mistreating Linc," Mother says, light as can be, as Father pads in and sits beside her. "On the heels of a brotherly squabble," she adds, a knowing glance over the rim of her snifter.

Father takes an impatient swipe at the wrinkled knees of his pants, baggier as he keeps losing his old weight. And he says, "It certainly doesn't really bother you, what Douglas said at the table? You enjoy pretending it does, that's all. But remember, it isn't your life that has fallen in on top of you. He can't really undermine you, can he? Don't look so grousy."

So I try not to.

"Oh, by the way, here, look at this," says Father, drawing something out of the inside pocket of his corduroy jacket. He moves his fingers around it like a magician and then uncovers, standing up on his other palm, a live twenty-two caliber bullet. "It was on the bottom attic stair," he says, "where it certainly didn't belong."

And I think for the first time in years of my rifle, shooting targets in the basement, firing down a narrow passage between oil tank and furnace, past shelves of paint cans and turpentine, pipes and ducts, everything to puncture, to ricochet from, and far at the end a piece of paper with a black spot, a nest of white ringlets, and sandbags behind. This is long past. The rifle must still be back under the eaves. Could there be a box of bullets too? Our snooping boys. Perhaps they found my badges too, my medals, my Marksman, Sharpshooter, Expert. But it's nothing to be ashamed of. The tiny black piece of lead in its gold shell on Father's palm.

"Could there be more where this came from?" he wants to know.

▼　▼　▼

It's dark, passing the old CCC sign at the edge of the village. These voyageur names, these villages, in Illinois French — Du Page, Des Plaines, Ardennes — tucked now between expressway and forest preserve, swampy woodlands filled in during the thirties, crosshatched into blocks, block after block. Before he learned to spell, Obadiah thought we lived in Our Dens, like bears.

"You know what Uncle Doug said to us when he went out the door?" Zephaniah asks the front seat. "He said: You poor little bastards!"

"But I didn't hear him say anything," I say.

"He did! He said: You poor little bastards!" says Zephaniah.

"He was yelling," says Obadiah, "so we came to see. We

were just standing there, and he said it to us, Poppa, like a whisper suddenly."

"That's the limit then, Iz. He's really started in on us again."

"But what's a bastard exactly?" Malachi asks.

"You know," says Obadiah.

"A kid whose parents aren't actually married, the impolite word for it," Izzy explains over her shoulder.

"But we're not supposed to tell people," says Malachi.

This is the subject Obadiah won't ask further questions about. He doesn't want to know anything about it at all.

"So does Uncle Doug know too?" Malachi asks.

"It's hard for someone who won't trust you to know for certain that something really didn't happen," I say.

"You mean a wedding," says Malachi.

"He's suspicious, that's all. He knows he wasn't there," I say.

And now they're sitting back. Who would break this sudden silence?

We're in the older section, rows of squat brick bungalows like ours, but here not interspersed with clapboard two-stories. An echo of Mother's scorn is creeping back into me from her first approach to us. How no one really lives out here, Lincoln! How in her earliest years there were gypsy wagons encamped in these swamps, their fires deep out in the dusky mist. And when the first green cars of the electric rail, with their red stripes, cut across this floodplain, who would have gotten off at the one dreary station? There's no geography out here, Lincoln. An appeal to my higher senses.

"I hope Spode wasn't too lonesome," Obadiah says to his brothers. "He could've come right inside at Grandmother's. We would've carried him to keep his paws dry."

I see in the rearview mirror Malachi whispering something.

"Oh yeah, and we could've shown him the attic too," says Obadiah.

I know better than to ask what they found on their explorations. They have realms I can only vaguely map out from hints and clues.

I try not to be the least fearful that they may have found that bullet, or a box of bullets, found even the very rifle itself. Does Isabel find it easier than I to trust, to wait?

I turn onto Jackson. It will take us the rest of the way across the village, home. We seldom talk on this last stretch.

A feeling. We are coming safely home, all of us together. No one lost, or stolen, or run over. Only in dreams I've heard screeches, screaming, I've found an empty bed. They never had bikes. A wheelbarrow is what these boys wanted. Ethereges are the ones with bikes, and they don't play together, they pedal off in traffic by themselves. We call them by egg sizes: Large, Extra Large and Jumbo. Jumbo and Large are the girls.

How is it I'm unsettled, until we turn onto Greenwood and I have seen the house still standing, dark in soft twilight, empty but for Spode, his chin on the arm of my blue chair? He will sense us before he's heard the car: Good is about to happen, not sure what yet, that aura, oh yes, and now that hum, that sleek sound in my ears.

▾   ▾   ▾

Sunday evenings it's tray food, in our separate corners whenever we want it. Izzy puts the stuff out. I will put it away. Between, it's up to each of us, quietly by ourselves. We need this lonesome time when the week is over.

Obadiah gets to eat at his desk, Izzy in bed. Zephaniah pretends to be camping out, cold, bundled up, on the front porch. I have my chair, naturally, and Malachi is in the basement with his tray, probably meditating on the coming week's excavations, cross-legged on the dusty floor, leaning his back against the furnace. He can never be too warm, Malachi.

What have I here? Ham with pickles and cheese on rye. Mustard, mayonnaise, nicely smeared together in swirls. I could become fat — already a little fatter around the middle — I could spread and puff out and get greasy. Douglas must still keep himself lean, his clothes must fit him right, must look like a good catch. Will he be caught again? But this tummy is getting uncomfortable. Good for cushioning Izzy, good for supporting this Ocean Floor book, but I'm not used to it. It comes and goes with the seasons, a bit more by this time of year, less in late spring.

Zephaniah is singing a campfire song to himself. He's pretending he's in Spode's river house, down in the rushes, the two of them, having a modest repast. I will have to come up with a new turn for the plot tonight. We've got him all set up down there with his secret dog life. What adventures might I have drift along the muddy stream? Zephaniah will only barely point the way for me. A canoe, he might suggest. But up to me to put someone in it, someone with intentions inimical to the peaceful life of Squatter Spode.

Our lowly life here. I take a long look across this dim room to the shadowy dining table through the archway.

It's set for Monday breakfast. Then we will become part of many other people's lives for some hours during the day that follows. Day that follows night.

▼   ▼   ▼

Obadiah appears to me in the dark in a picture of my own imagining and says, Poppa, do you realize what's about to happen to me? But maybe you have more time than you think, I tell him, you're only ten. Then I realize it did begin to happen to me at eleven, and, really, it had been happening all along, it was always there, straining, yearning, pulsing, puzzling impatiently over its odd impulses. No, I feel it coming already, says Obadiah, and I don't want it to yet, Poppa. This picture of him is febrile and opalescent. I don't find application for such words in waking life, but they lurk inside my mind, waiting to take their places with the sensations of the night, when time seems rather to rotate than to push forward. I think he's showing worry on his lips more clearly than the actual opaque Obadiah of daylight. He disappears and reappears. He's out of my reach. It's just his thoughts coming to me now, and then again a quivering picture of him in the dark of our bedroom, as if he'd gotten up to scribble a midnight thought at his desk and had somehow sunk, still lit by his gooseneck lamp, through the floorboards. But the picture comes closer, hangs over my side of the bed, so that I can see he's now even a little older, his gawky limbs have fleshed out a bit, there's a new fullness to his cheek, perhaps a shadow of light fuzz where his jawbone attaches and on his upper lip. His red pajamas seem too small on him now, and he sits cross-legged in the air on an invisible flying carpet from ancient Persia — that's how I imagine it. Can't you some-how stop it, Poppa? he's asking me. Can't you lock us up in here all day, not let us out? That's not what you want, Obadiah, I assure him. How can you know what we want! he asks right back. The three of us together! I don't want to go first! I don't want to have them noticing, curious, laughing about it! But they'll get there too, I say. Soon, Obadiah. And you said maybe I had more time! he says, fading back somewhat. No, it's only me pushing you ahead in my thoughts, I tell myself, you're not there yet, you don't even know about any of this. Come back, smooth gawky Obadiah. But the Obadiah keeps growing bigger and fading before my eyes. And now I'm fully awake because I want to stop seeing it. With a blink, nothing's there.

Izzy breathes gently beside me. It's my mistake to think she has only peaceful dreams. She has told me some of her worst. But from the outside, now, as she lies there, she calms me down, no matter what terrors may be forcing their way through her sleeping head.

3

IN TIME TO get most of them done, folded, sealed, addressed, weighed, metered, taken down for the noon pickup. But the others? One day more for those trusting customers. They must all be hopeful kinds of people. At any moment the yearned-for Standard Oil Illinois Highways, 1938, say, could show up in their mail.

It's my Imperial German flag making that flapping, brass eyelet clicking against the pane. Came off one of its hooks. Its brief stint doubling as Upper Volta is over now. What would Kaiser Wilhelm think of his stripes having come to represent the three branches of an African river? But Upper Volta's Burkina Faso now and they've a new design. Order from my man in Massachusetts when I balance out at week's end. If I balance out.

Monday, and I've started wondering if Galena will make an appearance after her doctor's. These short visits, these irregular visitors. Days may go past without a knock. If I stay late the super may stick his grizzly head in, to bleed the radiators before winter, or I'll get stuck talking to the mad-eyed potter down the hall. But a customer only rarely, a curious person off the street almost never. It's my dream to do it all by mail, to take my time, to imagine the faces of these far-flung map collectors, these flag enthusiasts — hearty? fusty? maniacal? — in their nostalgic or scholarly quests. It's only Gale, on her sisterly rounds, I'm ever glad to see, and I forget it's always on Mondays. Then oh yes, this may be one of her days. I'm not waiting for her, only reminding myself. And some Mondays she doesn't stop in at all, takes the expressway straight home. Her very bad days.

Stacks of warm manila before me on my desk, and all these destinations. It's a random task I carry out here, what someone happens to want, what happens to come in from my sources, what I manage to trade or happen upon on some prowl. I would not wish to be one of my customers, waiting for me.

What is it, in this big emptying building, small businesses failing season by season, mail piling up outside cold blank doors? A neighborhood of storefronts without customers, sealed-up warehouses without signs, vacant lots accumulating cement blocks, fenders. Uncle Bob's very used cars one block over. The last part of Chicago I ever would have seen. Has anyone I grew up with ever been within ten blocks of here? What Izzy and I discovered in our time of great exploration. We didn't go away to college. Well, she tried it, but back she came. Into our own unknown city, not these precise blocks but other blank blocks like them, out by the Circle Campus. And how would we have known, in high school, that it would become the time and place for us? Running somehow, down dark streets, alleys, gasping from whiffs of tear gas, I even bruised from some cop's blows at the height of the chaos, but we found comfort, a pack of comrades, exhilarated, amazed at ourselves doing what we were doing. Chicago seemed our infinite hideout then. Who was afraid of anything? And we ended up at a first-aid station. And then Izzy and I in someone else's bare room, held in each other's arms, the day's events having roused us so. What it felt like on a bare mattress in that big dark room, vague neon light hovering behind a grimy window. What glimpse of a new world in my imaginings?

The future still weighs on me. The more we have had of it, the more it is so and doesn't take guesswork. But that I am still hers and she is mine.

I'll have a grilled cheese with tomato and chat with Roland if he's in a better mood. Almost sunny enough to go across to the park bench. That's what I'll do if he's still grumpy. I hate sitting at the lunch counter, right there, a grumpy Roland blatantly ignoring me.

▼   ▼   ▼

I've sat up on the front of my desk to watch her. My tummy emerges in this position. She caught me in my socks, shoes lost somewhere under the desk.

Galena is vaguely scanning the road map spread open on the file cabinet. I know that smell of hers, lilacs out of season. "Remember our trip to Mammoth Cave?" she asks. "You should take your boys there."

A coldness from the window, ruffling the Kaiser's flag, swipes at my damp neck. I'm used to her bursting in, checking everything, keeping her chat up all the while.

"It left its impression," she says. "I'd like to take our

tribe on spring vacations like that. But Ed doesn't see why the Fox River isn't enough for anybody. Remember the stalagmites? Funny, Linc, what tourists we were! I mean the old kind. We'd all hop in the car, Father telling us kids to shut up, and he'd drive us all through Indiana and Kentucky, or else down to Springfield, New Salem, or all the way to Pere Marquette. We'd stop at every damn historical marker. And Doug would pee. The first state capital in Vandalia. The battle of Stillman's Run. U. S. Grant's house. Somewhere I've got my albums of black-and-white Brownie shots. Mammoth Cave, Spring Mill, Turkey Run. Remember tourist cabins before they had motels? And we rubbed Abe's nose at the tomb in Springfield. We were a normal little fifties family back then. So let's take a trip, says Father, out to Starved Rock or the strip mines to pick up fossils or to the Black Hawk statue for a picnic. He loved just looking at the countryside."

Gale's in her winter clothes already, black wool skirt and one of her Bolivian mantas, and high black soft boots. She has fixed her eyes on the polar projection I've tacked up over the map case, the whole world within a white Antarctic ring.

"That map dizzies me," she says. "Oh, and I had to help Mother prepare the picnics. And chubby Dougie slopping around the kitchen under foot. Of course you! Well, you and Father and the maps!" she says, giving my right knee a pinch. "See what comes pouring out after my fifty-minute hour!"

"Mammoth Cave, hmm?" I say.

"God, Linc, all these maps! They bring it back to me every time I come here. Mother with one of those old road maps spread out on her knees and you leaning over her shoulder pointing. You spent half your childhood leaning over the back of a front seat! Now why would anyone think we didn't have a happy childhood? You know, I can't get Ed to budge. Hell, why can't we get the oldsters to budge anymore! You should bring Father in here. Get him looking over your maps, looking for the highways the way he remembers driving them on our spring vacations. It's the interstates that have thrown him."

Gale's memories cause her to poke at me again, a chummy pawing at the gut, little sisterly. "Goose bumps?" she says with a chuckle. And she goes and shuts the window. I always feel a bit embarrassed but an odd relief too around her. Galena, my sister finally rethinking her past, fascinated.

"I get yapping with you like this, Linc, and then I'm running late all day," she says. When she first started dropping in after she got her doctor on the North Side I was afraid she'd want to set up regular lunches, that she'd have things she'd want to unload on me. But Gale has her own busy life to keep me on the periphery of, too.

"Nothing wrong with yapping, Gale," I tell her, fiddling at my buttons. I'm either too hot or too cold today.

"Sure," she says, "I suppose. It's seeing your maps mostly. Where do I ever go these days but my same old route? Mondays: home, shrink, gallery, school, home. Tuesdays . . ." She's leaning one hand on the doorknob, the other pulling at her boot till off it comes and she gives her toes a wiggle. "And Ed always says, No wonder, chief, it's Monday and you went to look at those damn maps again, no wonder you're so restless — you're so predictable! he says. So you don't suppose there's anything else I happen to do on Mondays? I prod him. Talk about defense mechanisms! And then we get arguing about not another weekend on the Fox River with your parents, Ed, please! It's hard being Mrs. Post, Lincoln. If you think the Peels are hard, try being a Post."

"It wasn't all that easy just being a Trace," I say.

Both boots off now, she passes by me with a quick cheek kiss. "Thank you, brother," she says and she's on her way to the U.N. display. "And speaking of us Traces, the former Mrs. Douglas Trace called. She says Sarie wants a Chinese flag."

"The Darrell Quong influence, I suppose."

"You've heard about Darrell Quong?"

"Have I heard about Darrell Quong!"

Gale is already flipping her fingers along the rows of small silk flags. "Oh that's right," she answers herself, "you were all up in Knollslea with the oldsters yesterday. Your Sunday duty, our Fox River Sunday — let's coordinate once, huh? Well, ex-sis Lauren caught me right when Ed was getting our tribe out of the house this morning. It's for Sarie's birthday. Could I pick one up from you if ever I got out this way? That woman! She knows all about my Monday shrink appointment, I'm sure. And so innocent and casual and aren't we just all still friends!"

"Taiwan or People's Republic?"

"Don't ask me," Galena says. "One of each maybe's best." She keeps flipping the small flags, not that she'd recognize either. Inhales, sniffs. "It reeks in here," she says. "Why did I close that window? Lincoln, your life needs to be taken in hand."

As she pulls up the sash with a loud rumble of counterweights, the black, white and red banner of two superseded regimes billows out, and the stand of small flags begins a hundred tiny flappings. "All I smell is lilacs," I say.

A dismissive flick of her long pale arm, Indian bracelets jangling. "So now I'm hearing from Lauren again."

"And why shouldn't you be?" I ask.

"Sarie doesn't seem to feel the wound has healed, Lincoln, Doug reports. Isn't it dismaying how children hold grudges for life?"

"The divorce was Sarie's first shot at a grudge, I suppose."

"And first times stick," she says. "It's only after you've had a lot of people to hate that you stop remembering so clearly why."

"Hate?"

"I don't know if I like being hated," Gale says. "I don't know if I like being hated by my niece. Am I? I am, I still am."

"You don't mean hate really."

Her face has gone slack. Look at the small creases near her mouth, near her eyes. Look at this tired sister of mine who never lets up.

"Sarie's very sad still, I know that much," I tell her.

"So how was she yesterday with her dad? Impatient," Gale answers herself.

"Yes."

"Bored."

"Yes."

"Children! I've had it up to here!" She slaps palm to forehead, immense exasperation, face wildly back in motion. A quick recovery. She's landed on my desk chair now, pulling her boots back on. "As if I turned Doug against her! As if I didn't just love my own little brother a bit more than his high-strung . . . It's so southern belle-ish of her! I don't care, Linc. But I never said a thing in front of Sarie! So where are these Chinese flags?"

I go to my understock, bent-up cardboard boxes, wrong lids, labeled wrong. People's Republic's below Chile. And Taiwan? Oh, in the illegitimate regimes box with Ciskei and Qua Quo.

"How did Douglas seem yesterday?" Gale asks, having whirled around on my desk chair, I notice as I emerge with the flags, and stretched her boots out on the windowsill.

I look over at the polar map. It's as if they'd opened the earth at the South Pole and peeled it out flat, but with the North Pole still a single point and the South now an infinitely thin line encircling all the continents and oceans. "What? Douglas, oh he emerged from a gloomy silence at dinner and went into one of his monologues: Izzy and I haven't given our boys the idea they can get anywhere in their lives. We've shunted them off, encouraged their oddity, we've kept them too close, we're even vaguely dangerous. Our refusal to bring them into the actual world — oh, and then when he was leaving he made some crack to the boys about their being poor little bastards."

Galena is thoughtful. She lifts her sharp eyes to me, expecting something more.

"Well, Mother and Father are entirely patient with him these days, Gale, because he's so touchy. First it seems Izzy and I'd taken Sarie for a walk just when he wanted to leave, and then when I didn't feel like all of us sitting through some movie Doug had fond memories of, the afternoon ended in a tantrum."

"Tiresome." Galena sighs.

"But it comes all from him."

"Boring!" she declares. "Waste of everybody's time."

"But Gale — "

"Oh, you and Doug can patch it up. Please! I don't take sides anymore. It's the oldsters we should be thinking of."

"This is what comes of your revisionist history? Gale, it's Mother's form of sport. She loves nosing out clues to our natures. She loves a good scrap."

So a cautious smile is growing on Galena's lips. Perhaps this won't turn out to be an argument. "But I wonder," she says, "if we don't sometimes overestimate the amount of fascination we arouse."

"Well, I'm not claiming that her fascination extends to actual concern!"

The slack face again. A skeptical glance in my direction.

So I go on: "It's Mother's constant search for continuing evidence of what she deduced long ago. I'm one way, you're another, Doug's yet a third. We all fit. Maybe she even planned us that way. Hmm?"

Gale sweeps her boots off the sill, and she's on her feet, brisk, all at once. She turns to the door, furling the Taiwan and People's Republic flags against each other, reconciled in one bundle. "You'd love Doctor Potts," she says. "Have a rubber band?"

But I don't, so she tucks the flags in her jauntily low-slung floppy purse. I reach and hold the door open for her. I have to say something more.

"Galena."

She turns, stylish, all put together, and looks back into my dusty unorganized piled-high office. The black, white and red flag starts flapping again at the window frame with the escaping hall air.

"Well, the fact is," I say, "I suppose it's just that I'm wearying of Mother's patience with the Successful Brother now he's on the skids so."

"Oh Linc," she says, "all right, it's true, I'll admit it: Doug's gotten away with being a total shit through this divorce."

For all the empty dim hallway to hear.

"And I'm sure it's true, Mother wastes too much of her time absorbed in all our lives. Ed and I, and our tribe, we've got enough going on to feed her ulcer all by ourselves. She needs her murder mysteries to calm her down after a dose of us. No, you're right. Presumably even Father gives us an occasional thought. But I'm trying to learn to treat them appropriately. Make them, for my own sake, into the parents I'd like them to be. It's remarkable what can be done to remake them. And that's why I'm trying to get them to take a long romantic trip somewhere this winter. Away. You could use a new curtain there."

"That used to be Upper Volta."

"Oh. But what am I doing still standing here talking to you?"

Quickest possible kiss. She's gone.

▼　▼　▼

I'm left to think about what? Of course Obadiah, who keeps coming to me now. I pull out my shirttails and wipe off the sweaty patch where my tail would begin if I weren't human, the sparse field of fuzziness there. A sisterly aura lingers about me.

And so, unbuckle the belt, Obadiah, Obadiah, tuck back in tidily, belt buckle clacking and clicking, Obadiah, Obadiah still. What is he trying to remind me of?

Tip of a shoe emerging by the desk leg. Other shoe way in under. I remember kicking them off. Here I am down on my knees on these creaky warping floorboards, dusty as ever, reaching. Aha, and a map that slipped down. Oh yes, this is the one that Mr. Battletree wanted of West Virginia. I knew I hadn't sent it yet.

Well, let me just sit down here and tie my shoes like a kindergartener. It's lonely work, old maps, and flags are lonelier still. And there's Isabel in her friendliest of shops, the chatty old duffers coming in all day. But it's what we each chose to suit us.. My poppa works in the city, I once heard Obadiah telling Jumbo Etherege when she'd asked him how come we only had one car. What kind of answer was that? Obadiah said the proud word: city. The city must be the place where you don't need a car, where you ride stately omnibuses down grand boulevards, where you disappear into granite towers, ride up in brass and mahogany cabinets, carpeted red, where you glide down marble corridors to your anonymous aerie with its wall of glass, its view to the beaches, out to the lapping waves and a horizon of distant gray. You could almost see Michigan from such an altitude.

But not from this Northwest Side brick block of faltering enterprises.

Obadiah hasn't come here since there's been the three of them. But nine years ago, those times I'd have him to myself all day, when he never cried, when he watched the flags rippling above the playpen. Could I bear to bring Obadiah here now? My lack of organization would dismay him, him with his infinite plans. What mess is this my poppa works in? Let's build more shelves. I'll get Malachi to get these maps in chronological order. Or alphabetical? Zephaniah, you take this dustpan. No, he wouldn't say it that way. Here, Zephaniah, he'd say, handing him the dustpan, you know what to do. Subtle, complimentary. Then he'd point to a tumbling pile of maps. Malachi, you're good at sorting things. That's all he'd need say. And I'm going to design a wall of shelves with dividers and cubbyholes and map drawers. And then planning would take weeks, and then building would take months, and Obadiah wouldn't have to think about anything else for a while.

Not his fears that came to me in the night.

But soon enough. I remember how I, behind locked bathroom door, standing on toilet seat, watching close-up in medicine-cabinet mirror, and it grew longer and longer, almost by the week. Does Obadiah lock a door? They still shower together. Their L-shaped attic allows for no privacy. We should rearrange, put Obadiah the furthest in. We should hang a curtain for him, and he could emerge, his new private self, new growth modestly tucked in underpants, in T-shirt sleeves. Just switch him with Zephaniah, and Malachi can maintain the middle corner. Malachi, neither first nor last.

Shyer with me, Obadiah, these days? Have I caught the sense of a constant secret? That I'm beginning not to know him as well. Yesterday at Mother's, never quite in the room with us. An embarrassment. And a touch of the young brave, of the initiate.

No.

Let me think instead, eight years back, nine, that yellow plastic adjusto-seat from Izzy's shop propped up here on my desk, and now I kneel up to the edge, squinting, to see it again. There's the little fellow, I've got him to myself. Izzy's got the new one at work, that helpless lump of Malachi. And here's our Obadiah, about to outgrow his adjusto-seat. He wants to sit and watch me work. He doesn't want to be down in his playpen despite the pretty flags. So I sort the maps at hand. I address mailers. I open the day's mail and let him chew envelopes. But how can I work? Better to kneel here and observe the slight gestures which contain every gesture to come. The little hand that will draw plans, dig tunnels, grasp and stroke the thing that's only a mere nozzle now, the hand that will one day reach cautiously under angora sweaters for a touch of breast, the very hand.

I could have stared at him for most of an afternoon. That was Poppa at work in those days.

And here Poppa is, same room, some same flags even, some same maps. Some that have come and gone and come again. And this floor warps more and the grit collects in cracks, and the window grime, and it's all unknown to that boy. I wouldn't bring him here.

So let me look at West Virginia. Let me drift about in it. West Virginia has so many towns with funny names. There's Duck, Big Otter, Little Otter and Gip. Up the road to Shock and Stumptown. Joker, Speed, Kettle, Left Hand, Quick, Pinch, Given. These are towns. Couch, Scary, Hurricane and Tornado and Cyclone, Sod, Mud, Leet, Wewanta and Uneeda, Cuzzie, Midkiff, Fry, Crum, Van, Hazy, Man, Cucumber, War, Elbert near Filbert. Only crossroads. I'm lost here. Rock, Bud, Odd, Ramp, Smoot, Duo. Droop, Auto,

Sue, Muddlety. Clay, and didn't I just see Sod? Bergoo! Czar!
Replete, Pumpkintown. And all in one state. Elk, Job, Rio,
they like three-letter towns down there. Paw Paw, Omps,
Points, Shanks, Glebe, Hundred, Rock Lick, Reader, Wick.
I love this map. These places are real in this world. More:
Trout, Unus, Mud, didn't I just see that?

▼   ▼   ▼

I'll pop into Roland's, something for the bus ride, a tummy
expander of some sort. What's left on this pathetic rack at
this hour? Lemon-cream minipie. Tastier warmed up.
Should I really?

"Don't stand there gaping," says Roland. It's not his true
grump, it's his everyday jolly grump to regulars. There's
that cold cream distributor. He's been giving her a hard
time.

"Could you microwave this for me, Roland?"

"Presto," he says, and seconds later, while I'm watching
for the bus out the steamy window, "Change-o!"

I dig in my pocket.

"How do you like my lady friend?" Roland asks as I pass
him a dollar and he says, "Thirty-five."

"Hi," I say to the woman in the yellow uniform, tight
over a pinkish bra. A bulging red freckliness inside there.

"Oh she's a heartbreaker!" says Roland. His litany, how
women won't give him the time of day. "It's this old belly
puts her off," he humphs as I head into colder air, eying
the building directory, white letters clutching black felt
strips: L. TRACE'S OLD SPAM. I'll leave it. Roland will
only switch it back again.

Dark out earlier now. The bus down the block, and my

pie's nice and warm. Well, it was also a way of getting the change I'll need switching lines.

Some thought about Galena's ragged look under all that bustle, all that resolution. One of her not so good days?

▼　▼　▼

They're early to bed tonight. Yesterday I think they were up late planning something, whispering, after we thought they were asleep. Now Obadiah's eyes are sunken. He's not at his desk, he's on his bed reading over what he's scribbled microscopically in his pocket notebook. Malachi and Zephaniah won't even touch that notebook, and Izzy and I don't either.

Malachi under his quilt now, no light at all. Asleep? Thinking?

"Malachi?"

Nothing. Zephaniah is barely propped up, waiting. He doesn't like my idea of switching corners.

"See, these are my cracks in the wall," he tells me. "That's the stream going by Spode's house, and that's the lagoon where the bulrushes and cattails are, where the plaster came off."

Obadiah didn't want to switch either. He expects to be stationed at the top of the stairs, their guardian, their protector.

"Where were we?" I ask Zephaniah, settling beside him. He's feverishly warm.

"Spode saw that canoe."

"That wasn't a good place to leave you. How did you ever get to sleep after that?"

"Yesterday was a big day" is all he says.

I'm thinking about that canoe. It was just the very bow of it emerging behind the rushes, slow, silent, from the wide bend in the muddy stream, aluminum like a mirror, catching the sunlight that had broken through the rain clouds at last.

"So Spode saw the canoe," Zephaniah coaxes me, but sleepily, then I shake out my mind and hope for words:

"At first it didn't seem in any way remarkable to Spode. He was going about his business, setting out water bowls and a tray of Woofles for Scoper and Iola, whom he'd invited for a snack on that soggy morning. But that silvery glinting in the corner of his eye annoyed him, and he shook the brown fur of his topknot for a better look. It was moving too slowly, thought Squatter Spode. He was used to the church outdoor clubs that paddled by occasionally, singing the sorts of songs he never heard in the precincts of his own people. Hymns, Iola called them. Her people had recently abandoned the Slavic church of their forebears for a hymn-singing one over in Des Plaines. But in this silver canoe all was silent, not even a ripple proceeding from a dipping paddle. Something deep in Spode, his sense of auras, unnerved him a bit. And so he stood at the window of his house among the rushes and watched, nose a-point, as the silver bow lengthened and three figures, in army-surplus rain gear with dark hoods obscuring their faces, appeared amidships, like a grouping of cold bronze statues, gaping at the reeds and saplings on the banks. A tremble started in Spode's forepaws. Like walking sticks, to support them ashore in this marshy wilderness, three long metal tubes stuck out at different angles from the green statues, one skyward, one leveled at the bank, one pointing along the tops of the rushes. I mustn't move, thought Spode. I must trust in my camouflaging autumn-hued fur, with my eyes like dark berries."

Zephaniah's hands, both of them, on my wrist, gripping, hot. I'm getting all this from that murder mystery of Mother's I was flipping through yesterday. Time to wind it down for the night:

"But this time, at least, Spode was in luck. The canoe glided by, a matter of yards from where he stood. Spode had learned about shotguns from Scoper, who had been to the North Woods with his master. Those shotguns, those still-wet green hoods, those faceless ones, all slipped beyond his bank, and now he made out, on the far side of the canoe as it turned the next bend, a paddle ever so gently worked by the figure in the stern, his weapon lying crosswise on his lap. Bad times, thought Spode. But the sun was asserting itself in the eastern sky. The day would be warming up and drying out. You can imagine with what relief he heard the approach of his friends. First, Scoper's lightfooted bounding, then Iola's bearlike lumber through the brush down to the edge of the water. Much to be told, over water and Woofles. Good to have friends who'll come out in all weathers. Lucky to have been that close to danger, looked on its shadowy face, and then to have seen it gliding past, smaller and smaller, down the peaceful stream. Such were Spode's thoughts as he went to meet his friends."

Is Zephaniah asleep? The grip has relaxed, the sweat has evaporated, cooled him. Those delicate lashes. Murmuring.

"What?"

"Malachi said about Mrs. Schnell again," he barely says.

"Said what?"

"Said about her coming around again. You know."

"And talking to him?"

"She never comes around to me though. She smiled at me in the hall. She doesn't know who I am," says Zephaniah, his last word.

Malachi a silent lump over there. Even Obadiah's put his light out. I creep by them.

4

Izzy's there on the edge, tan terry-cloth robe on the green quilt, reading another Sinclair Lewis. Doesn't notice she's picking at her toenails, peeling off a ragged bit, flicking it onto the rug between her side of the bed and the wall. That's one place I seldom set foot, only when I vacuum back there. Those toenail scraps suck right up, but it's her worst habit.

"Hi, toenail," I say.

"Hi, corn," says Isabel, a wince in her eyes at being caught. "Oh I'll gather them up," she promises.

"It's not the toenails, it's the picking them off, sends a quiver up my spine."

"Ooh," she says, "nice!"

"There's quivers and there's quivers," I say, untying my robe, settling in, feet too cold to pull off my socks yet. Let everything under the covers get warm and a little sweaty first. It's gone awfully cold in just a few weeks. Time for puttying windows. "What you giggling about?"

"World So Wide," she says. "I love these books no one reads anymore. I feel like they're mine alone."

"It's your own bedtime story, Iz," I say.

"How much longer before Zephaniah stops insisting on his?" she wonders.

"In the spring, when he's nine, then maybe. Malachi got his till he was nine."

"But Obadiah stopped earlier."

"Yes," I say, "but as Zephaniah rightly points out, Obadiah's been able to keep listening to both his brothers' stories. He got the best deal."

"And always will," says Iz.

Now she's warming under the covers too. I feel her knee encroaching. Bone by bone we move toward each other as we talk. It's one very slow approach to a hug. Dwell on each new point of contact.

"Well, so what's happening now with Spode and friends?" she wants to know.

"Oh not much. Remember that night I told him about the hunters and he was so scared, grabbing onto me?"

"Remember his nightmare?" says Isabel.

"But it's hard making it a story without something like that, Iz. Malachi always liked the scary parts. He'd stare at me with his eyes buggy. And Obadiah used to ask those terrible questions: What happens exactly when you break your teeth off? Or: How long before the body rots?"

I sit up, leaning forward on my knees, a chill passing over my back as the sweaty flannel separates from my skin. Izzy turns, relaxing pressure on my hip, my calf.

"Linc? These past weeks, there's a worry in you. I see it passing across your face. It doesn't show for long."

"Probably," I say.

"Nothing is happening?"

"Nothing has happened. Could anything happen, as such? Must be something way under. Quiver-producing."

"Lean back here."

"Mmm."

"Warmer?"

"Warm again."

"Hi, buttocks," she says.

"Hi, crack."

"Linc, there's this having to see Mrs.Schnell tomorrow."

And of course she's right, it's been on my mind.

"I could go with," she suggests.

"But who'd open the shop? I'll go. You can see her the next time."

"The next time?"

I look at Isabel. We don't know. Instead, a deep breath, a sigh, a shrug, a squeeze, a nuzzle, warmer and warmer.

She's whispering in my ear: "So then what did happen in the Spode story tonight?"

"I had him and Iola go on a romantic little picnic," I whisper back, "and the hymn singers paddled by. Iola howled along and Spode admired her dulcet tones while regretting the deflection of his more secular intentions. Of course we all know Spode no longer has the capacity, but Zephaniah hasn't quite put two and two together. Very attentive to my words though. Keep your ears open for him noticing how dulcet — "

"Is that something flashing outside?" Izzy asks aloud, lifting her head off the pillow. I follow her glance to a shimmering corona outlining the front window's shade. But silence.

We both get up, stumble over, flip the shade up. It's a car on fire across the street, two houses down. A car in flames, black steel frame through yellow fire. Parked in front of whose house? The bluish house. No one in sight. Whose car?

Iz runs to the phone. I don't know why, I run upstairs to the boys. Asleep, no, where's Obadiah, his bed's empty. Spode slams into me as I'm coming down. Something's up, excitement, danger. This way, Spode. He bounds back to the living room. I bang down into the kitchen, Izzy on the phone, light from open basement door, on around, dining room, places set for breakfast, flick switch by the archway. There's Obadiah, red pajamas leaning over the back of the couch, staring out.

"No, I can't see it with the light on, Poppa," he says. Spode's licking at his toes.

"Momma's phoning."

"I was asleep. It was flickering in my eyelids," Obadiah says.

Now a distant siren. "Someone already called, Isabel says, barefoot, wrapped in robe and a dark shawl I've never seen. "Obadiah!"

"Look at those fat Everages in bathrobes out on their lawn, one, two, three," he says.

Sirens. Now Malachi will be down.

"Go tell him it's all right. Quick. And tell Zephaniah." Obadiah doesn't want to stop looking, but the flames are dying. Nothing exploded. Is that sirens or a crying kid? "Oh hell!"

"All right," says Obadiah, moving too late.

Flick switch. I'm on the stairs, and there's Malachi at the

top holding his brother's hand. Zephaniah is between cries. He sees me, Izzy and Obadiah behind, then Spode too.

Family on the stairs.

▼   ▼   ▼

"This was our expiatory feast," I say of our nocturnal bananas.

Isabel looks at me with tolerant skepticism. She's thinking I don't quite know what I mean by expiation, but she's used to that. In the candlelight the boys are slurping the last sugary milk from their bowls.

"We'll leave the bowls, need them in a few hours again," I say. I hear the heavy fire truck pulling off, up Greenwood.

"But Spode didn't get a feast," Zephaniah says.

"Get him a Woofle," Malachi proposes.

At first Zephaniah seems afraid to leave the table, to enter the dark kitchen and find the treat box by far-flickering candlelight, but he goes.

"He was afraid in his bed, he was all shaky," Malachi whispers to me. Private information he's been saving till Zephaniah left his side long enough for him to impart it.

"You were good with him," I whisper back.

Izzy's slow sleepy stare has rested on Obadiah. Is she looking for something? He's acting glum, fiddling with his empty spoon.

"Were you down in the basement?" she asks him. "The light was on behind the basement door," she says. "I was standing there on the phone, and there was that yellow light around the edges, and suddenly I thought our furnace had blown up, the whole neighborhood was on fire, spontaneously. That's how my mind works," she says.

Obadiah hasn't answered. He winces. "I thought I turned it off," he says to himself.

"Oh let's go to sleep," says Izzy. "All of us. Spode, calm down, this isn't morning."

It's Obadiah who gets up and grabs onto Zephaniah, gets him whirling and giggling. Izzy is moving in a dream, passes right by them, shawl dragging. Oldest and youngest cavort around her and off up the stairs, Spode in pursuit. I'll let him finish out the night with them.

Now here's Malachi's hand.

"Poppa," he whispers.

I squeeze back.

"Obadiah goes down there in the night."

"When?"

"I hear him go sometimes."

"Well, that's all right, he probably has things to do," I tell him. But alone? I think. Oh. Already?

"Sometimes he leaves us," says Malachi on the first stair.

▼   ▼   ▼

I am shown in by a bleached bespangled woman from the outer office.

"Mrs. Schnell," she says with her bright nails sweeping toward an open door.

There she is, behind a metal desk. A bare room, pale yellow paint slathered on cement blocks. Mrs. Schnell looks up — small woman, black tight curls, heavy eyebrows — doesn't stand. She has a stare.

"Mr. Trace, correct?"

We shake, she swivels her chair my way as I sit across the little room. No window, but glass bricks aglow from the outer office. There's nothing of hers here, there's nothing at all, only her briefcase and her winter coat on the hook on the door I closed behind me.

"Malachi's father."

"And Obadiah's and Zephaniah's."

"I haven't had the opportunity to meet with them," she says. "I go around the township to all the schools. There are too many kids to see individually. It's their teachers who aim them my way."

"Aha," I say. I'm going to let her do the asking.

"Are you the primary-care parent?"

An icy phrase. I know what she means by it, but I'll act puzzled.

"Are you with the boys most of the time?"

"We both are," I say.

"Aha," she says. Is she imitating my aha? And she's sitting with her arms crossed like mine. Her theory about relaxing me? But she does stare. It's a liveliness under those thick eyebrows. I don't dislike her, but I'm armed.

"You didn't explain in your note what you were concerned about, Mrs. Schnell."

"Well, as I say, the concern originates with the teacher. And then I try to be of help. It was the scratches on his forearms in this case. They caused Ms. Wishart to look more closely at your boy. Of course, nine-year-old boys have lots of scabs and bruises, but there were other things about Malachi. Interesting name, by the way. He certainly never gets scraped up in recess. He'll only play on traveling rings, up and down, back and forth, all by himself. If it's a game of pom-pom, he lets himself get caught right away as if the game didn't matter, and he never goes on to help catch the others. Same with bombardment on rainy days in the gym."

"It's nothing to worry about, I hated recess too," I say. "I used to watch his future mother across the playing field. You bring back memories."

"Where was that?" Mrs. Schnell asks, and when I tell her, "Aha, Knollslea, quite a different sort of community," she says. "So you're from Knollslea! Not many ex-Knollsleaites in Ardennes. Out here, Knollslea is only a glimmering mirage."

I didn't mean to allow her to do this. Now she's retracting her stare. New tactic. She's musing.

"Perhaps your boy feels out of place here?"

"He'd feel more so in Knollslea," I say. "Little kids are said to have their own private computers in Knollslea," I add for a laugh.

Mrs. Schnell snaps her chair up, raising a finger. "That's the other thing!" She's flipping through a folder. "Ms. Wishart says he becomes listless and dreamy over the computer. Yes, you're the one with the computer problem. Traveling rings, scabby arms, computers. Ms. Wishart was trying to put those themes together. The boy's very verbal. Look at this."

She hands me a yellow scrap. In a familiar hand:

	MALACHI TRACE			
	AAAIE MLCHTRC	TRIAL	LAME	MALE
	~~MILE CHART~~ ACA	TRAIL	CRAM	CLAM
A CLIMATE ARCH	~~A CLAIM CHART~~ E		MALACHITE	~~CAR~~
	ACCLAIM HEART			ARC

"He does that all the time," I say.

"You'd think he'd take to the computer," she says. "How many fourth graders can rearrange letters like that?"

"His hobby."

"Or even know those words!"

"I tell them complicated bedtime stories, complicated words, Mrs. Schnell. They're old-fashioned boys."

Mrs. Schnell swivels, tilts, muses, taps her pale fingertips together. She's puzzled. She wants me to see how puzzled she is. Those eyes are working under her heavy brows. My heart is thumping. I must say something to throw off her timing, what I know she's building to. She's rather attractive.

"Mrs. Schnell," I say, "I'm sure you must speak to a lot of neglectful parents. I'm sure you have your way of coaxing them. But we aren't what you thought we were. We're not what you'd call a case. I don't mean to throw you off, but we don't care if our boys don't excel, as you might put it, at pom-pom or have any reasonable use for computers. Malachi likes using his own head for rearrangements, and as for the traveling rings, they build up his arms."

"His arms!" Mrs. Schnell says, grabbing the folder. She's caught up to me. "But can you help me out a little?" she asks. "What was it he said? Here it is: says he fights with brothers. What are his brothers, clawing puppies? See, Mr. Trace, I do speak to neglectful parents, and I do speak to overprotective parents, and I also speak to abusive parents. But how do I ever get to the bottom of it? You can't imagine how people disguise their behavior. I can only trust that eventually it will show, somehow, and somebody will see it."

"Oh you and my damn brother!" pops out of my mouth.

But she doesn't look offended. Milder now, almost. Waiting for me.

"My brother's very conventional, I mean. He's just been

divorced. He's tender on the subject of child rearing. Always blasting me. His own daughter has practically everything she wants."

Mrs. Schnell shuts the folder on her desk. She rearranges her pencils. "You know, Mr. Trace, I've always been one sort of an activist or another. I tend not to follow the establishment line any more than you. I may not be quite as much of a Luddite, but I'm not trying to force the modern world on your kid."

"Aha," I say.

Then she looks off. I'm looking at the yellow paint on the concrete blocks above her head, not at the blocks, at the paint, the very paint on the thin surface.

"Myself, I grew up in a privileged suburb too," she says. "Well, Evanston wasn't quite Knollslea, but close enough."

"Mrs. Schnell — "

"Just call me Sherryl. We must be about the same age. We probably marched in the same protest marches in the old days," she says, peeking into her folder again, the upper corner. "Can I call you Lincoln?"

What can I say? Her openmouthed smile has given her a different sort of face suddenly.

"Let me give you the bigger picture. There's been some vandalism here at school," she says. "Not serious, but worrisome. I'm the one they come to. I'm supposed to know how to cope. Why would a youngster set fire to a wastebasket? Or tear pages out of library books? Why would a little girl's jacket get soaked in a toilet? Vandalism, neglect, abuse. It's on all our minds. We don't want to see unhappy children. The vandal and the victim, really, in children, they're not so different."

"But my sons get somewhat scratched from the excavating they're doing for their mother, who has plans for a garden in the spring. I'm sure some other teacher will soon be tipping you off to the scabs on Obadiah's knees or Zephaniah's muddy fingernails."

That comradely open smile again. "Your boy, your boys, they fit a certain profile, that's all," she says. "It's my job to look out for them."

"Well, thank you for that," I say and make myself add: "Sherryl."

"But would it trouble you if I asked to see your wife sometime?" She lifts the folder's corner once more. "Isabel?"

Clever woman to catch me off-guard.

▼   ▼   ▼

This unfamiliar late-morning bus, lurching emptily, the Northwest Side flashing by, and I'm not noticing cross streets. Fat black woman driving just me, and the face of Sherryl Schnell appearing and disappearing before my eyes. Warm, icy, confiding then suspicious, swiveled this way, swiveled that. She was putting me through something. Izzy will do better. She'll get talking about the old duffers who come into her shop and how little they have and how a knit hat already worn a dozen years that's lost all its shape becomes a treasure to an old man at fifteen cents, and the young mothers without husbands who come trading in constantly outgrown baby clothes. Ought to appeal to her vaunted activism. But it mustn't be on one of Izzy's bleaker days, when she's feeling a bit lost.

What if I had known this Sherryl in what she called the old days?

A familiar hue, the pink pennants of Uncle Bob's Used Cars whipping in wind. My stop coming up.

▼   ▼   ▼

To slow us down. Izzy's phrase, ours. We haven't let ourselves be deflected.

I'm pouring into a green-stemmed goblet, this moment that seals the working day. And I'm carrying this goblet, catching the faint sunset in each window, and now as I settle into my blue chair again, I'm resolved into the midweek world. A sip does it. We're circling back to our places. Izzy on the road now, aiming straight home. Spode is listening somewhere. And there is detectable activity below, a scratching, a scraping, a murmur, a plop of earth.

I see into these sounds.

Obadiah is on his knees, reaching the bucket down to smaller Malachi who lies in a narrow cavity clawing at deeper soil. Zephaniah directs a flashlight, stalwart, dutiful, never bored. The yellow light glances off Obadiah's crooked elbow and off the curve of the bucket handle and slips down along Malachi's flank to a spot of black earth. His pale left hand, cupping a tiny load, snakes backward like a Cambodian dancer's until it tips into Obadiah's bucket, soundlessly. And after forty-odd passes, the bucket swings on Obadiah's arm into the fullness of the beam, and Zephaniah, putting down the flashlight, grabs the silvery bucket and empties it into the wheelbarrow behind him, up in the basement proper, and that is the occasional plop I think I hear. But during that emptying, his older brothers are in darkness, and they close their eyes not to feel darkness so frightfully. It is only a few seconds before the empty bucket returns and the light flashes again into their narrowing tunnel, but it is almost the reason for what they are doing, I think, that blind time, image of what is to come, when their finished work has all its turns and twists, the burrows for taking naps and the chambers for sitting, and all the sides are packed solid and through touch alone they can find their familiar way.

I sip. I have imagined all this.

But will it hold them as they grow? Are they engineering for their future statures or do they imagine the passages from chamber to chamber need never be more than wriggle spaces? I sense them — eighteen, seventeen, sixteen — sitting in their own dark domain, perhaps a snuck bottle of wine passed unseen from lips to lips and Spode, old and slow, curled across three pairs of big bare feet. And perhaps Obadiah will once lead a girl in with him, for the first time, to a nest he's made, an old foam pad, a blanket, packet of rubbers conveniently stashed, some system of signs to brothers, a shovel crosswise on the wheelbarrow, do not disturb. What will she think? Trust him? That the earth might fall in on her? Better out under the open sky, where you can shout and it gets lost in the wind, down by the lagoon, in the rushes, not here right under his parents, every breath bouncing off the black walls. No, says Obadiah, it's safest here, earth insulates us, we are absolutely alone. Poppa's tummy keeps him out, and Momma's afraid. She won't even peek in at the opening. Obadiah knows how Izzy must dream of them perhaps smothered in there, her boys lost under a collapse, too late to dig them out.

The brief tick-tick of Spode's toenails on bare floor, crossing from bedroom window to window behind couch. He knows what must come next.

▼   ▼   ▼

Sitting, waiting, I must've gone off dreaming of Izzy and this old man. A picture of her welcoming him, the one looking for the wool hat, into the small room behind the counter, her gently tapping the door shut behind, and her climbing up that step stool so he could put his old mouth onto her. Up slid her skirt, bunched at the waist, her panties pulled down by him when she told him to. And it was right at the level of his head. Oh Mrs. Trace! he said before he leaned his lonely face in between her thighs. My pleasure, she said. His arms felt upwards, it was hard for him, arthritically, to get to her nipples, but it was no sacrifice for her, no charity. She found it glorious. That old man was feasting. He wanted her so much, scarcely believed his luck, nibbling, licking, stroking, pinching.

Oh, she's home. Spode in ecstasy, a welcome such as brothers seldom give long-lost sisters. "Spode, Spode, Spode, Spode," she's saying, packages falling from under elbows. I leap to assist.

"If you'll allow us, Spode," I say. A particularly serious kiss, aroused by that strange picture of her on the stool.

"Lincoln!"

"Mmm," I say.

"Well!"

Spode has made a sudden frantic descent to the basement. "We know she's home, Spode," grumps Zephaniah's faint voice through the heating duct. But before that dog makes it back upstairs, to let us know he's let them know, we're behind our closed door. He'll wait patiently. We'll be quick. It's come as some surprise to both of us.

There's Isabella already sprawled. She's full of laughter and delight.

▼   ▼   ▼

"And then I spelled acclaim," Malachi goes on, the story of his triumph. "They all thought it had one c, so I won. And then came the spell off, me against this girl, Patty Kopczynski. It was sacrilegious."

"So?" says Obadiah slicing his pile of spaghetti all one way and then crosswise before he'll eat a bite.

"She thought it was sac-religious because it had to do with religion."

"So?" says Obadiah. "That's what it is, sac-religious."

"It's sac-ri-legious," says Malachi.

"It's got to be sac-religious."

"It's like sacrilege," I put in. "You wouldn't say sac-re-lige, Obadiah."

He thinks about it, fishing for a manageable forkful.

"Well I won," says Malachi.

"Wait a minute!" Obadiah gets up and scoots into the other room.

My middle son and I exchange a glance of silent confidence. We hear the big dictionary slam shut.

Obadiah, with a gesture of capitulation, reenters. "Point!" he says, tapping Malachi's head.

"What's sac-religious?" asks Zephaniah.

"It's sac-ri-legious! Don't you get it!" says Malachi.

It's Obadiah who answers: "It's when you do something

to hurt what somebody else believes in. Well, you know how Christians believe in the cross somehow? If you took one out of their church and snapped off the top part so you could use it for a T square. You know my T square I have on my desk, Zephaniah? Well, that's an example."

"You know what a kid at school did in recess?" Malachi asks us all. "He took and crucified a worm with pins on a Popsicle stick."

"A worm doesn't have arms!" says Obadiah.

"You can still crucify him."

"We keep our worms," says Zephaniah. "When we find worms, Momma, they go in the wheelbarrow, so they'll be good for your garden in the spring."

"But sometimes they get sliced into two worms by mistake," notes Malachi.

▼　▼　▼

"And so began the Journeys of Spode: the stubby pram, caulked, repainted, stocked with Woofles, both maple and strawberry flavored, and a big bag of generic Kibble, with Iola astern ruddering and Scoper and Spode each at an oar. Iola has struck up one of those hyms but it comes out doggy. 'Marching as to war!' she howls. It helps the rowers keep rhythm. And soon Spode's river house has disappeared around the bend and they are upon unfamiliar waters with only the 1959 Chicagoland map for guidance. Spode had slipped it out of an open drawer in his people's kitchen. 'Let's see here: From this meandering backwater to the wider Marne, from the Marne to a narrow canal to the North Branch, and on.' "

"But Spode's home asleep right now downstairs, Poppa."

"This story isn't happening today."

"But Spode's always here. He never goes."

"This story's happening in the future, Zephaniah."

"But I'll worry about him."

"You can worry when it happens," I say. "Now he's safe downstairs with Momma."

"But what about then?"

A muffled voice comes from under the mound of quilt on Malachi's bed: "It's a story, it's supposed to be exciting, it's better that way."

"But how am I going to go to sleep?"

"Shut up!" comes from around the corner. Obadiah is trying to concentrate on what he calls his blueprints because he uses blue pencil.

"But what if more hunters come paddling the other way?" whispers Zephaniah, close to me.

"Hunting season is over," I say. "It's the middle of summer in the story. Everything's slow, drifty, lazy. It's too hot to think of anything. You know that feeling?"

He's satisfied.

I pull up his extra blanket, get a squeeze of my hand, lips too tired to kiss me back.

▼ ▼ ▼

I climb in beside her with my Travels in the Steppes. From below I hear the furnace shut off. Thermostat turned down, a last warm air current drifting up past us, dissipating. Now it's our time.

"This Saturday night we'll set back the clocks," she says, checking hers to see how late it's gotten. We don't usually sit up in the living room so long after the boys are asleep, but I didn't want to talk about Sherryl Schnell here in bed. I needed coffee and lights.

"Now you seem sad, Isabella," I say, reaching over, pulling her near.

"Tired. All that exercise before dinner!" she says.

"No, but sad."

She reaches tightly around me and feels the stomach I'm not used to having as much of.

"My brother called," she says. "He and Billy want us for dinner on his birthday. Us, no kids, a grown-up evening, if you can call it that, two weeks from Friday."

I hum acceptance and turn my hum into a human purr.

I remember hiding with her in the little woods behind school, in recess once, during kick the can. They expected you to be brave in that game, leap out, free the prisoners. We huddled like this in a scratchy thicket. I remember feeling her bare arm like this. Eleven years old? Didn't usually get to play in the same games, boys and girls, anymore. Then a long year of watching from far off, of thinking up our future lives.

"Izzy, what are you sad about? Mrs. Schnell?"

She doesn't want to tell me.

"But Mrs. Schnell and Malachi and her suspicions?"

"I don't think so," she says.

"Still worried about that car fire last night? We'll try to find out something tomorrow. The Ethereges will know something."

"I was thinking more of Obadiah somehow, his being the oldest," Izzy says, close against my pajama top.

She too.

"We fell in love, Iz, when we were Obadiah's age, didn't we? Then, or a year older."

"In love," she says.

"Yes."

I'm squeezing her to me, soft in my arms.

"In love," she says again, amazement in the word. "But if Obadiah won't find it in this world," she says and catches her breath, tight. "Or if he won't give it, Lincoln. If he won't give it. That's what it is."

"But and if," I say, trying to comfort her.

5

THIS SILENT ELEVATOR into another world. I don't see such broad smoothly shined surfaces in mine. Here nothing is wrong with anything. Their two rooms would buy a dozen houses of ours. It excites me to be here, but I can hardly allow that. If the world would be all clean glass, brass, steel, and freshly shampooed carpets down long airless halls. No, but there is air here, filtered, pure. Where does it come from?

Which door? G. Peel and W. Sharp. A silent button. A miniature peephole.

"Linc, buddy!"

He's always huger than I'm prepared for. "Billy," I say, shaken in the enthusiastic-kid grip.

"Only me. Birthday boy's probably stuck in traffic. Where's Isabel?"

"I came over by bus. She had a parent conference."

"Not the Three Holy Children in trouble!" he says, leading me into the tight spareness. A huge travel book, a fish tank bubbling.

"Oh yes, they're a burden, Billy."

He grabs me around the shoulders and says, "Someone's got to do the rough job, Dad."

Does he know I'm joking? I know he's not really thick, just hard rubber solid — but soft-faced, twenty-four.

"And how's it going for you so far this season?" I ask.

"They're letting me play every now and again, so things must be going good, right? No chance Monday though. I'm used to the bottom of the barrel by now. What would you like to drink?"

Billy's got himself an ale, so I say, "Ale's fine."

Two new white couches since I was here last, the white carpet, it's so comfortable. And the clawless gray cat slipping off into the bedroom. Then that glass wall of the view of buildings of lights. We're up in the air. Billy's in his sweat socks. He sits diagonally from me. An eager nodder and smiler.

"All this white wouldn't last with our mud trackers," I say.

"Nice, huh? Gabriel's on a white kick. Hey, so catch me up on those boys. I mean to be getting them down to the locker room finally this season."

"They're hard at work as usual on their tunnel," I say, but it's hard for me to get up to Billy's pitch. He's so encouraging, squeezing onto his ale bottle, staring at me.

Then he goes right on: "You know, way back me and my buddies had, well, not a tunnel, but a clubhouse? Down by the river back home?" He makes questions out of things to be sure you're still involved. "I swear if that isn't where I learned half the bad things I know," he says and hoots a good one.

"Aw, you don't know any bad things, Billy."

That gets a second hoot. "So come on," he says now, "what about Shadrach, Meshach and Abednego? Uncle Gabriel's going to want the full report. Did I ever tell you, first time I met him, there were those three little faces peeking across his desk at me from his photo cube? And I didn't want to get too nosy. Those had to be his kids, right? I figured he was just divorced like everybody else up here." Now Billy's serious: "You know, Linc, what I tell Gabe is if it hadn't been for the Three Holy Children, I might've figured him out sooner. They kept me from jumping the gun, see. But somehow I just went on stopping by the head office. Hey, you catch us last Sunday?"

"I read about it," I say, not remembering who won. I know he won't pursue it. He'd never want to embarrass me.

A key in the lock, brother escorting sister.

"Look what I picked up in the elevator!" says Gabe's voice.

▼ ▼ ▼

Billy's chopping furiously in the kitchenette, bright-striped jersey stretched across broad back. Izzy has put down her empty ale next to Caribbean Vistas.

"That Mrs. Schnell was one suspicious lady," she says just to me. I lean closer. "There've been more incidents, as she calls them," Izzy says. "I told how we'd already heard about the worm crucifixions. Then it came up how Malachi studies extinct animals, and she seemed to find that morbid, as though it implicated him somehow. She was swiveling around on her chair and flipping her files and eyeballing me. I eyeballed her right back. Malachi isn't capable of dousing girls' jackets, I said. He doesn't hate little girls." But Izzy's conviction only sharpens the vision of our boys spiriting my old twenty-two from their grandfather's attic to the backseat of our car. I can't help picturing these things.

Gabriel comes back from the bedroom no longer the dapper CPA but in socks, jeans and one of Billy's practice jerseys. "Who's minding the nephews?" he wants to know.

"They're past the sitter stage, Gabe. They can call the Ethereges if they need to," I say.

"Remember when I used to sit for them?" Gabe says. "I'd buzz all the way out from the North Side, just to sit. I mean I loved it, since I was always one lost dude on Friday nights."

"Pwoosh!" goes Billy at the sizzling wok.

Gabe remembers the Ethereges too, those fat kids hanging all over his convertible Rabbit.

"We had some excitement on the block, Gabe," Izzy says. I only half-listen as she goes through the car fire story yet again. Mrs. Etherege, who never had much to say to us, is still coming by daily and pounding our knocker with the latest. The arson investigator came around and talked to her. The car belonged to that teenager across Greenwood, Rodney T-something-ending-in-wicz. The kid was in tears. His Barracuda!

"You guys planning a trip or is this a decorator item?" I ask, picking up the travel book. Gabriel arches an eyebrow in my direction. "Well, Gabe, think how far you've come since your coffee table featured a stack of empty pizza boxes."

"When the season's over, we're off to the Caribbean!"

shouts Billy. "Barbuda? Nothing but sand. We're going to
fry our hides!"

▼   ▼   ▼

Three ales have set Gabe reminiscing over his sitting days.
"Back then Obadiah was always so dead serious. He
thought I was way too goofy for an uncle. I embarrassed
him I think. Malachi didn't seem to mind as much. He'd
go along letting Uncle Gabe dance him around on his shoulders and maybe I'd get a giggle out of him. It was Zephaniah
I could really crack up. Because he was the baby, he was
supposed to. Not Obadiah though. But I know he liked me
a lot in his premature adult way. I certainly never had to
run herd on them. Some baby-sitting!"
   "And you never had to tell them they couldn't watch
TV!" Billy says, switching us all over to wineglasses for
dessert.
   "I never told them they couldn't do anything!" says
Gabe, still slightly amazed at the fact.
   "Me they had to use heavy religion on," says Billy. "Read
your Bible, boy!"
   "No, all we did was slow them down a bit," I say. "We
didn't have a method."
   "We took them with us everywhere, always," Izzy adds,
"to work and shopping and never even expected they might
complain, which they didn't."
   I notice we're both sounding a bit smug. "They didn't
feel we were doing it all for them," I say nevertheless. "The
point was they were lucky to be allowed along."
   Gabriel and Billy are looking fuzzy over there behind the
candlelight.

"What do you say, Bill, shall we adopt?"

Thumbs up from smiling Billy in the glow of the candles.

When we talk about the kids I feel proud and glad, but I don't want to say so. I want Billy and Gabe to sense it, not so as to regret being childless, oh maybe a little but not in any severe way, but to make them understand what we have, because sometimes I feel a hint of scorn, from Gabe at least, a sense of us being caught and of his clean glassy freedom.

A pop from the kitchenette. I didn't even notice Billy getting up, and here's champagne flowing. Izzy's reaching for her bag where she has the orange foam-rubber dice we're giving Gabe to dangle from his rearview mirror, not that he will, but she thought of his period of delayed adolescence when they came into her shop. What else does Gabe need now anyway? Finally he has what he's always needed.

"All right, birthday boy, close your eyes," Billy says, and he grabs the matchbox from the table and fades off into the darkened kitchenette once more.

A scratch. Tiny glows begin quivering, floating toward us out of the darkness, casting soft light on Gabriel's dark, somewhat thinning hair.

▼   ▼   ▼

Maybe it's too much champagne. Why are we even still talking like this?

"Yeah, it's possible, everything's possible," Gabe's answering me. "We'd have to do it sort of under the counter is all."

"Foster kids, there's thousands of them," says Billy. "The team does a lot to benefit foster kid programs, you know, inner city, Fresh Air Fund, young black kids. Hey, your dad loves that, Izzy! It's good your brother has a macho job with the team or he'd never get away with our lifestyle."

The soft-pawed cat has hopped onto my lap, purring. Spode will detect her and run his twitching nose all over my pant legs.

"Us dads do what we can to keep in charge," I say, "but it's not all that much in the end."

"We're just dreaming," says Gabe. "I'm not ready to be any kind of dad. Even half of a dad."

"More cake?" offers Billy, tipping the last flat drip of champagne to me.

Their cordless phone burbles. Gabe tilts dangerously back to reach it from the fat arm of the couch by the fish tank.

"Yes, he is!" he proclaims. "Oh hello, Lauren. Should've recognized your voice." He reaches me the phone between the guttering candles.

"Lauren?"

I alone am hearing this, her slow drawl somehow frantic.

"I called you at home, Lincoln, and Obadiah said you were at Uncle Gabriel's, so I tried to find him in the book, but I ought to have known he's not listed, so I called back and Obadiah had the number of course. Now earlier I happened to call Douglas and he said Sarie wasn't with him and he didn't know anything about it, but Sarie said she was going to her father's. But Douglas said she'd switched plans a week ago, and now I'm in a panic. You can tell, can't you? I wouldn't usually have called Douglas, it's not in our agreement, but I felt sheepish about Sarie. I've been getting on her nerves something awful lately. I just wanted to apologize to her. Oh, thanks for those flags, Lincoln, by the by, I never thanked you, I appreciated them so much. I guess I'm pretty distracted lately. Well, then I called that boyfriend of hers, and I could hardly understand a word Mrs. Quong said. I guess Darrell's usually out on Fridays anyway. It's probably nothing to worry about, but Sarie took her backpack and I snooped in her room and there was a lot missing. More clothes than she'd ever need for only a weekend. But her schoolbooks were still sitting there! And she'd raided the pantry for snacks. It's only been a couple hours now. But I didn't get home when I told her I was going to. I had a dinner date. It never even occurred to me. She was on her way to her dad's, from what I knew. She had her fare and everything. Am I overreacting? Oh Lincoln! I'm calling you because it's you she talks about being the person in the family she trusts."

▼   ▼   ▼

The expressway has curved us up and out, through Park Ridge, across the Marne, and now on toward our exit in our aging Falcon. I must concentrate. I know I'm not sober.

And Gabe and Billy back there, better off without any small companions snuffling through the night with them in their tight condominium. Tomorrow Isabella and I will once again be taking note of the slight broadening of knobby shoulders, the three heights steadily encroaching on ours, and be hearing our own big words properly employed. It dissipated before we got to school, said Zephaniah yesterday of the fog I'd seen envelop their shuffling little forms that morning as they reached the corner of Jackson.

Off to school. More Sherryl Schnells will be down upon us, one after another, in time.

Really, it's in your kids' hands, Isabel said firmly to end the evening. It always has been. We're their observers only. Gabe was holding his cat to keep it from bolting down the hall carpet when we were all standing at his door ready to leave. But I'd think it would make parents crazy, he said, not knowing what exactly they're responsible for. What did I do? What did I cause? That's how Lauren must be thinking, isn't it? And she doesn't even know if Sarie ran away. Maybe she's at the movies. Maybe she left a note and Lauren hasn't found it yet. But what did she do, Lauren's thinking, and what didn't she do?

And what did Douglas do? I added.

Billy was looking so crestfallen. He was worried too, and he's never even met Sarie Trace. He ran away once himself, he said, from all that Bible: I took off down the river in my rowboat. I didn't get all that far. But ever since then I knew running away was mostly what I was going to be doing from then on.

I never tried to run away, said Gabe, stroking the cat to keep it still in his arms. I never even snuck out at night like Izzy did, he said. I was always home. In my room. Maybe I'm where your boys got their nesting instincts from. I see a lot of myself in them. Izzy was the spunky one in our family. Weren't you, Iz? And she always had Linc. I can't hardly remember before the time Linc was part of our family. Izzy and Linc off tearing up the city and me wondering when I'd ever have a life out on my own like that. And listening to Dad and Mom griping, afraid as hell to ever be a disappointment. And staring out at the lake for hours on end, watching the waves fall.

We all shook our heads. There were our old lives. Run away. Tear it up. Stare. Wait. Izzy and I descended in the elevator, silence in us and all around us.

Now in the car she's watching the road in her persistent reverie.

Still not sober. My hands grip the wheel tight. "Our Dens coming up," I say.

▼   ▼   ▼

A dark and silent house. Is Spode upstairs asleep with them? In place of a story.

All three tucked in without us? Isabella's creaking up the stairs, but I see Obadiah's blue scribble safety-pinned to the back of my chair.

Momma and Poppa:
   We went to the Everages. Uncle Doug called and got us all scared about Sarie running away. That was after Aunt Lauren called again. You know it all. Jumbo E. said we could bring our dog and watch TV over there with them so here we go. It's a monster movie, but still.
                                   Love,
                                      Obadiah
                                      Malachi
                                      Zephaniah

Signed by each. "Damn my brother," I find myself saying.

PART TWO

▼ ▼ ▼

1

"BUT IT WAS sometimes difficult to tell if they were turning north or south, west or east. Spode wasn't even entirely sure, always, of left or right. And so in this intricate maze of streams and canals, of lagoons and as-yet-unchanneled marshy places, the voyaging dogs found themselves somewhat lost. It wasn't the permanent kind of lost, where you despair of ever finding your way home again, but rather that tiresome and annoying kind, such as when the biggest and gruffest of Spode's people makes the wrong turn on the way to Aunt Gale's house and the whole family finds itself in Highland Park and not in Lammermoor at all. Those first days of rowing had been so exhilarating. Remember how they had come alongside that flotilla of Christians and learned to sing their peculiar hymns? Iola, of course, already knew most of the words, but she couldn't exactly explain their meaning to Spode. 'You simply have to Believe,' she told him. 'But it's preposterous,' Spode said once they had rounded the next bend, 'to hear grown people, people much larger than my three smallest, imagining some sort of Lord has been to pay them a visit, announced his message and tootled off again leaving them in their same ghastly predicament! There's something wrong with the whole idea,' declared philosopher Spode. 'It sounds like a tremendous excuse to get us all off the proverbial hook.' Iola wondered if she should argue the point. She'd always been told that Believing didn't get you Off anything. But she decided to concede Spode his point. It was true, she had to admit, she'd never noticed these Christians behaving in any way that distinguished them from other human beings, or dogs for that matter. 'It strikes me,' Scoper announced, 'that all creatures are out for themselves and you won't convince me otherwise, Iola.' And Spode knew then that they were in for another dose of what Scoper termed his War Stories, all about those crisp autumn days in the North Woods, in his master's van, with shotguns and brew and a plethora of rude jokes, which Scoper would insist on repeating, despite Iola's urgent protest. 'Please, not the one about Moose Dung Pie, Scoper, please!' "

"Tell it again, Poppa," says Zephaniah squeezing my tum.

These cold nights he always cuddles closer, tighter, and he wants a longer story, a story that goes on and on, with the dogs chatting happily amongst themselves, as though nothing untoward could ever happen to them. That's why I've got them entangled in this mess of waterways, and with luck I can keep them there, rowing in circles, for months. If only Sarie would come home!

"I'm not telling the Moose Dung Pie joke again. You know it by heart. I heard you telling it to Extra Large when you took Spode out yesterday."

"Extra didn't get it," says Zephaniah.

"Well now, where were we?"

"Tell it."

"No, no and no. Anyway. Hmm. Yes, they had encountered some interesting types in their travels. Greetings exchanged with those friendly dark-skinned fishermen on a high bridge they were gliding under. Scoper had muttered something about them being blacks. 'Well, you're a black too,' Spode observed. 'But my skin underneath is sort of dusty blue-gray,' Scoper made clear. 'It's the skin color that makes the difference, not the fur.' Spode got the feeling Scoper had reason to dislike those fishermen, but he couldn't figure why. Granted, Spode in his three seven-years in this world had seldom seen people with such dark skin, for he lived in a village of Czechs and Poles mostly. That's what Iola had called them. He'd seen the Poles. They stuck up along each street and had wires strung along them, and some of them had lovely moons that began to glow, automatically, at dusk. But he wasn't sure where the Czechs were. The sidewalks, actually, were sort of like Czechs. Long rows of Czechs. That was it! You see, in some ways, philosophically for instance, Spode was very sophisticated, but when it came to human sociology, he drew a blank. He took his people one at a time and liked them that way."

I think Zephaniah is finally saturated. Now his face has a sleepy glow to it, the eyelids puffy. Will he let go of me if I ease away from him?

"I love you, Poppa" comes out of his drooping lips.

Why do I feel this tremor gurgling through me, and this

pressing of water at the back of my eyeballs? I'm filled with my children.

They won't run away.

▼   ▼   ▼

He wasn't at his desk, and only Malachi was in the bathroom, zoologically examining his teeth in the mirror up close. Well, Obadiah's down here, red-pajamaed, in my very own blue chair, a jangle of colors.

"Where's Momma?"

"She's dyeing in the basement," he says. Then grins. "Dyeing things for the shop. Get it?"

"Ha-ha."

"Good one, huh?"

"Why aren't you upstairs, Obadiah?"

"I never can sleep till late at night, Poppa. I can only sleep in the mornings. Then I can sleep all day."

I know this is a sign. This is his body churning itself up, then flat exhausted. The solar system is wrong for his age. He needs more of a Martian day.

"Have you appropriated my chair?"

Silently he slips off it, flings himself facedown on the couch. I take time settling, sorting the sections of newspaper on the side table, straightening the stack of atlases.

"Been looking something up?"

"I was trying to find where Sarie was," he says.

Of course that's what's on his mind, and why he stays close, lingers in a doorway long after saying he's got something else to do. And all I can see suddenly is Douglas pacing through his echoing house, beating his fists at the walls. Or flung helplessly on his couch too?

"They know she's all right because of her letters," I say. "We shouldn't worry. She's visiting Aunt Lauren's sisters. She's on her way to see another one now."

"Malachi told Mrs. Schnell how his cousin ran away," says Obadiah.

"He did?"

"Well, she wanted to know about our family. You know what she said? She said what does your older brother do to get your goat? So Malachi said he didn't have a goat. Ha-ha. But she meant about us fighting all the time like he told her we do. He makes up all sorts of stories for her, Poppa. Like the time we were wrestling and I got the door on the furnace open with the flames in there and I was trying to push his whole head in."

"Obadiah!"

"Poppa, he's just making it up."

"But don't even think up something like that. You'll give me a nightmare."

Obadiah grins into the couch pillow. "She believes Malachi," he says. "And then he told about Sarie, and she wanted to know what school she went to in the city. I bet she's going to check up and see if he's telling the truth."

"There's been too much of this Mrs. Schnell," I say aloud.

"And he told her our family was odd," Obadiah says.

"Odd?"

"You know, Poppa."

"But why is he letting her ask him these questions?"

"He's not scared of her anymore," says Obadiah, tilting his soft cheek against the couch pillow. "He says she's nicer to him."

So she's worming her way in, I think, and that's worse.

"Of course he doesn't ever really tell her things," Obadiah goes on. "He likes making up stuff about our lives. How we never go on vacations and always have to be home and can't watch TV."

"You can watch TV."

"Poppa, I said he was making it up."

But now Obadiah's got me wondering. We should plan a trip to Mammoth Cave in the spring, or at least to the strip mines to find fossils. Why do I never think of trips, of showing the world to our boys? I want us all to stay home.

"See, Malachi wants it to sound like we've got problems. He thinks it's funny to see how Mrs. Schnell looks so concerned, like when he told her our dog won't let anyone in the house. Everyone on our block is scared of him. He bites the neighbor kids on their fat bottoms. Kids didn't come for Beggars' Night because of Spode."

"The Ethereges switched costumes and came three times!" I say.

"Poppa! Don't you get it? I said Malachi was making it all up."

But this is coming from somewhere, I'm thinking.

"And he made it all up about Sarie, all about how she was probably a prostitute now because she was a very sexy girl and she used to show her bosoms to us for a dime."

"Obadiah!"

"She didn't, she didn't!" he yelps. Brief hysterics. He's never said the word bosom out loud before. Now he bends one red-flanneled leg up and pulls the foot down till the heel bumps his bottom. Then kicks back against the couch arm, whack, whack, full of restlessness.

"You're not going to get mad at him, Poppa?"

But I don't know. Do I like it, his telling lies to Sherryl Schnell? Yes, I like it. I want him to mislead her, to force her hand, to discombobulate her.

"No," I say, "I won't get mad."

"That's what I like about you, Poppa," says Obadiah in the voice of a sudden adult. "You and Momma ask us about something and then we tell you. But you never make us stop."

Now he's burying his face in the pillow, totally flat Obadiah, narrow as my palm. Then, like bacon being turned, he's flipped on his back. I hardly saw him make the move. Ceiling staring. The red pajamas against the brown couch aren't so jangling. Yellow glows from the reading lamps at either end, and here beside me my green glass shade, warming the atlas stack.

"Did you find a place Sarie was?" I ask.

"I found Bardstown, Kentucky. I found Leesville, Louisiana, where she went now. I found where she said she's going, Pas Christian, Mississippi, Poppa. But then I was just opening to any old page."

He's looking at the ceiling as if he saw a huge white map on it. The Pole? I almost see lights in his eyes, almost fire. He's moving his hands, as if tracing outlines on the plaster. Then he flops his arms at his sides. Head tilts my way, cheek to brown pillow.

"Actually I like our family," he says.

And now he feels like talking, so I watch him with a coaxing in my eyebrows, and he talks.

"Uncle Gabe used to sit for us, remember? He'd listen to us telling him about all our projects, and he'd watch us.

He never told us to do anything. Now he's happier because he doesn't live all by himself anymore. He said he doesn't even drive his Rabbit fast like he used to. He said he got afraid suddenly of having an accident. He wouldn't want to die now. You know, if you look close you can see through his hair, Poppa. He said he's going to take us to the locker room after a game to see Billy. Billy thinks that'll be a big thrill. See, Uncle Gabe knows we'll go anyway, for Billy. What I mean is, Poppa, he knows we wouldn't really want to spend a whole Sunday at the game, but I mean he knows we'll do anything for him."

Obadiah is getting frustrated trying to explain this, but I nod him on.

"That's why I like our family," he says. "See, our family, Poppa, isn't the same as your family or Momma's family. It's both of them. Uncle Gabe's our uncle, and so's Uncle Doug our uncle. See what I mean? Even if Uncle Doug thinks we're poor little bastards. Remember once we were at Grandmother's and we went exploring in the attic with Sarie? That's when she got so mad telling us about Uncle Doug. So we started doing imitations and that got her to laugh."

"Doug imitations?"

"See, Poppa, the thing about Uncle Doug is he's so jumpy. It's harder to do him than Uncle Gabe. Here's Uncle Gabe: So Obadiah, hmm, how's school, dude? What do you say! And Billy's in the background going: Hey, Shadrach! Buddy!" Obadiah puts on a moronic grin.

"Billy's not that dopey," I say.

"But Uncle Doug, Poppa, here's him: Oh sorry. Excuse me. Oh, hi kids. Now what was I saying? Oh yes. Well, I think so too. Sarie, go do your homework. Dammit, can't we just relax for once like a normal family? What did you say?"

He's got him.

"Or else he gives up," says Obadiah. "Like this, Poppa." Obadiah starts staring buggy-eyed at the ceiling and looks terribly sad to me. And that's Douglas right now, I'm thinking.

"But you like him too?"

"He's part of our family, Poppa. Some of our family I wouldn't really like that much on their own. But see, even Aunt Lauren's still in our family. It doesn't matter if she got divorced. She was there all my life. I always wanted to sort of lean up against her skinny arm so she'd know I was there, like at Sunday dinners. Grandmother never had her be like her own daughter there. That's what I mean. But she's my aunt anyway."

He's pleased with himself, with what he's telling me.

"You know what?" he says. "I was thinking how Grandfather's like Malachi's toy dodo bird, getting thinner all the time with stuffing coming out. And Gramp and Gram, Poppa, they're like old potatoes. They get so lumpy and brown with little things growing off them."

"Obadiah, what are you talking about?"

"You want to know how Gramp and Gram aren't like Grandmother and Grandfather? Grandmother and Grandfather are like flat tires going phwoosh and Gramp and Gram are like old potatoes. Grandmother's more like a bike tire, I mean, being thin already, but Grandfather's like an old inner tube, you know, going blblblblblb."

It's a farting noise he makes with his lips against the couch pillow.

"But what's this about potatoes?"

"You know, Poppa, how those potatoes are in the bag on the basement stairs. Sometimes little green things grow out of them in the dark. You never noticed how Gram has these lumps and bumps and Gramp has them too, under his chin?"

"It's old age," I say.

"And they're brown and speckled, and they're getting bulgy."

I'm wishing Izzy would come up from her laundry and slip in and hear all this, but I can't call her, I can't break this spell. I'm seeing her parents as potatoes, hovering before me, potatoes nestled in their chairs at Troutbeck, perched over the gray rippling lake that smoothens toward the slate horizon.

"Poppa, you're having a dream."

▼   ▼   ▼

"Isabel!" I can barely hold it in. "Isabel!"

She can't hear me over the dryer. The whole basement is whirring, furnace too, and water running in the pipes for Obadiah's shower.

"Still at it?"

"Whoo!" she says, turning from the ironing board. She hadn't seen me. She's got dusky green curtains draped over the clothesline, sock rack, washing machine. "Well, they were so putrid I had to do something," she says. "It took four loads. Nicely made curtains, but who'd want them in sick orangy pink? The shop perpetuates enough bad taste as it is."

I slip my arms around her now she's back ironing, and I start to tell her: "I've been having a long talk with Obadiah,

Iz. He was so talkative suddenly. Suddenly he had so much to say, about everyone in the family."

Izzy smiles, keeps moving the iron. She's listening with my mouth up close to her ear in this loud basement.

"I wanted you to hear it too. I wish I could've written it all down. He started off being funny, about how Gramp and Gram look like lumpy old potatoes."

Strikes her funny. Twinkling eyes and a curl to her lips.

"But then he got quite serious. Trying to explain somehow the different ways he feels with Peels and Traces. He wondered why Gramp and Gram are so loud always and Grandmother and Grandfather always move so slow and talk so quietly. So how come Momma turned out quiet and Uncle Doug loud? he wanted to know. He decided some of what people do is opposite of their parents on purpose, and some is exactly like them, they can't even help it. He's never puzzled things over with me like that before. It was wonderful, Iz."

"Good I wasn't there," she says, putting aside the smooth curtain and reaching a wrinkly one off the washing machine. "It was maybe the right moment for him with you alone," she says.

"He's so smart, so interesting, he keeps surprising me, Iz. He said Grandmother never acted like Lauren was her daughter but he thinks who Grandmother likes best is Uncle Ed. She acts like Uncle Ed is her son, more even than me, he said, or Doug. Grandmother acts so proud of Uncle Ed, he said. She doesn't act proud of her real sons. Oh and he went on and on. He's got Gale's kids all figured out. They'll do anything. They actually like it. They're so happy, they don't know they're stupid."

Izzy's grin, her eyes. I let go of her and start walking around the basement. Somehow I can't contain myself. "But it was so exhilarating, Isabel!"

She finds me amusing.

"But talking to my little comrade up there, Iz — that's what he seemed like, a comrade-in-arms. Then I told him he had to go take his shower. I wanted to savor all he'd said."

The dryer shuts off with a thump. Now it's only the furnace. The water in the pipes has stopped whistling.

"They're coming to the age we're going to like best," Isabel says. "Old enough but not too old quite yet. It'll go by quickly."

"But I'm going to keep him talking," I say. "How can he stop now?"

"But maybe not always to his parents," Izzy says.

Now I'm over at the furnace and can't resist lifting the latch and swinging open the door to the roaring fire. That picture of Malachi's head being wrestled into it. Better to look in now than to dream it. Before my eyes the flames tumble and roar.

"You didn't turn the thermostat down?"

Just beyond the furnace there's that hatch of theirs, plywood pulled over their entrance. The wheelbarrow standing there, a few small clods of dirt and pebble that didn't dump all the way out. The bucket, the flashlight, a crowbar, some picks.

"I'd better go turn it down."

"Wait," she says. She's pulling the last tangled curtain out of the dryer. I go to touch her.

▼   ▼   ▼

Come in, Spode. Must I drag you? I will not stand by this cold door. You've done what must be done. You've discerned the significant messages on leaf and stump. No need to sniff about for the finer points. See, the light's out now. A beef and cheese Woofle for you, if you'll only come. Oh. There's a moon. That bare tree's like a silver spiderweb suddenly in the blackness.

▼   ▼   ▼

All quiet.

Then, "Oh no!" says Izzy. She's peering out the front window. Did I hear a car door? "It's awful late for Doug to drop in," she says.

I grab my robe, but before I even get the belt tied our knocker goes whack, whack, loud enough to wake the boys. Spode scurries about with welcoming squeals, and he doesn't even know who it is yet.

When I unlatch and open the door, there's Douglas in his orange slicker, peering cautiously in at me, soft-eyed.

"I'm sorry," he says, the apology deflected by eager Spode. "Go back to sleep, pup. Well, I took the chance there'd be a light on." One hand keeping the dog from jumping, the other reaching out to shake my hand. He's unsteady. "All right, I'm a bit soused," he says. Tears have appeared in his eyes, and he staggers into a hug with me. A beer smell. I hug him firmly around the shoulders. The rubbery slicker and he feels rubbery inside it. He holds on longer than half a minute, gulping against me. Little brother.

"We're glad you came, Doug," Isabel says, following as I guide him into the living room. "Tell us what's on your mind. What do you hear from Sarie?" He sinks into the middle couch cushion with Izzy and me on either side helping him ease out of the slicker. Wagging happy Spode adjusts to our inattention, retires to his spot by the heat vent.

"It's more than I can bear," Doug says. "I know she's all right. She sends postcards. But I feel too sorry for her. I can't think of her traipsing about down there so homeless and lonesome." He looks each way, at Izzy, then me, needing us. "I've talked to her a few times," he says, then sudden fury crosses his face. "You know what it turns out to have been? We finally found out. It wasn't me or Lauren at all, it was goddamn Darrell Quong! The little bastard was toying with her. All the times she said she was out with him, well it was usually the whole crowd of kids and she kept hoping he'd get serious with just her, but he got serious suddenly with some other young honey instead and that's what he told her one night. There wasn't any hope for her. She'd wrapped herself up in that twerp! How can a kid treat another kid like that? She wasn't telling Lauren, she wasn't telling me. She was too proud, Lincoln. She made such a deal to us about what a great thing it was, her relationship. It's so mature, she said one time. Dad, we're not deceiving ourselves. We're very realistic. We both like the security, that's what she said. She gave me a whole lecture about kids her age these days. But it was all out of wishes! There wasn't anything. Darrell Quong was off porking someone else!"

Douglas seems soberer now that he's unloading. He loosens his red tie, his collar button, but his reddish hands tremble still.

"Want some coffee?" Izzy asks. He looks gratefully at her. Spode follows her into the kitchen. I put my arm around Doug's soft shoulders the way I got used to doing last year during the divorce.

"Linc, see, I always come to you. We have our fights, but still."

I pat him, calm him. "Have you asked her to come home?"

"With every sentence I utter," he says.

"What does she say?"

"She couldn't bear seeing her friends or Darrell. They all know why she left. She made some grand scene about what a loser she was. It's as if she'd stood up in front of her friends and immolated herself. They all knew how she was counting on Darrell. It was sheer humiliation. I can see doing that, feeling the only way to pull it off is to make it even worse. You think I'm just fooling, she was saying. I'll show you! This isn't pathos, this is tragedy! I'm going to be extreme!"

"Maybe it was to get Darrell to come around?"

"Oh no," says Doug. "She knows him better. She told me on the phone Darrell wouldn't go for that approach. Once you've lost it in public, Darrell won't have a thing to do with you. He's the arbiter of style in that school."

"That's it then! Have her come home and go to her old school and live with you, Dougie."

All the lines of Doug's face pull up tight. I've said the worst impossible thing.

"Because," he begins. Tears are coming. "Because she did the same thing there last fall. We didn't know. That's why she won't see her old friends when she comes up on week-

ends. I have to take her to movie theaters in other towns
and restaurants they'd never go to. After the divorce, she
made this big announcement to her friends, see. Her life
was wrecked. She was going to live like a cloistered nun,
she said. She was never going to have anything to do with
other kids. She was going to dress ugly. They'd never see
her, though. She was going off to live with her mother and
never make any new friends."

Isabel has come back with a tray. "It's instant," she apol-
ogizes.

"Fine," says Doug. "Give me the big mug."

An odd assortment of shop items. The Century of Progress mug goes to Doug, for Izzy and me small green-glass
teacups. I stir in milk and sugar with a Québec Je Me Sou-
viens spoon.

"I was telling Linc," Doug says, "how Sarie's so proud,
how she won't go back on what she's once said, how once
she's felt humiliated in front of her friends she'll never let
them see her any other way. I mean it's not really stub-
bornness, is it? It's pride somehow."

▼   ▼   ▼

We bedded him down on the couch. He kept saying he was
going to leave, but Izzy told him she wouldn't sleep if she
thought of him back alone at his house with these
thoughts. Or worse, still driving around, I said.

So I'll just lie here, me and the dog, farting through the
night, said Douglas. He was feeling better after talking,
even being funny now. Izzy brought in another blanket.

And after more talk of Lauren and her desperate life —
No, he said, he wasn't desperate like that. Of course, it's

easier for a man, he said. Real easy, said Izzy, giving him a hug. And tears again, but winding down. After all that rocky life with me, he said, Lauren thinks she's going to find someone better for her. And I'm thinking about Sarie. All I'm thinking about is Sarie. Oh all she's thinking about is Sarie too, now. Give her credit. Here we are, two of us thinking only about Sarie and we can't talk to each other without everything coming up again.

Sarie is all right, Izzy reminded him. But at Thanksgiving, I'm thinking about going down there and getting her, Doug said. Just go and get her. Lauren says I shouldn't. But I can't bear it. Every night I dream of driving. And that got him talking about how little he's been sleeping, and how his research is going to pot. Narratives of Reconstruction, or whatever it is now.

But what'll your boys think when they see their hungover Uncle Doug passed out here on a Thursday morning? he asked us before we went back to our room. They've never had breakfast with you, I said. They'll consider it an event. That made him smile. I didn't want to say they've been worried about him too.

Now all these sleeping bodies around me. Izzy a softbreathing lump, three boys above us out like lights, the exhausted dog, and Doug raspily snoring across the hall. If I could float into some half dream.

"Linc?"

"Mmm."

"I'm not asleep either."

2

IT WAS A goat, not a dog, prancing in a small patch of green meadow, flashing white over dandelions, in and out of clumps of tall grass. Malachi in pursuit but convulsed in giggles, not really wanting to catch it, diving and missing, rolling on the green. A sunny dream.

No, not a dog. Spodelike, puppyish, but definitely, clearly, a goat. And was that even Malachi really? I was almost Malachi myself for an instant.

And a memory somehow of when we first got Spode, and the boys had tried to find a name for him. Malachi, too young to know why we couldn't, wanted to call him Boner because he liked bones. But anyway Obadiah found it a stupid name. Then how about Spode for a name? suggested newly talkative Zephaniah. Because Izzy was always joking that if only the crockery at her shop turned out once to be genuine Spode we could all retire. Spode he is! she declared, picking up the wriggling puppy under his arms with one hand, he was so small.

This is the Sunday we have to go to Troutbeck. Damn.

▼　▼　▼

"Every time Uncle Doug stays over now I let him have my wart bowl for oatmeal," says Zephaniah, slurping the sugary milk he's spooning up.

"That's kind of you," says Izzy.

"Remember when you never wanted that wart bowl and now it's your favorite," Malachi points out. "Poppa, it's only because Uncle Doug says it makes him barf."

"No, but it's the way he says it," Zephaniah explains.

"Bwllrrawrff!" goes Malachi into his own smooth bowl. Obadiah exchanges a tired glance with me while his littlest brother guffaws with delight.

Our secular Sunday.

"Is Uncle Doug coming today though?" Zephaniah asks, settling back down.

"You boys like it now when Uncle Doug comes," says Izzy.

"I like it best when he sleeps over," Malachi says. "I can hear him like the garbage truck through the floor. I like waking up in the night and hearing him go fnroormpf down there."

"Uncle Doug's funny in the mornings. He pretends he's still sleeping," says Zephaniah, "he pretends he's bumping into chairs. Is this my fork or my spoon?" Zephaniah says in a hungover-Doug voice contemplating his knife.

Doug has this new admirer, it seems. It's done him good. I'm trying not to feel displaced. I've looked on calmly at my small son on his knee, my authority undermined by a demonstration of all the digital tricks Doug's watch can do.

A slow sip of hot sweet morning coffee. I'll leave Izzy and the boys to toasts and juices, go settle with the paper in the other room. Izzy's pink arm there, gracefully across the back of Malachi's chair, his head bent over, buttering.

Coffee steam rises to the green glass shade, condenses, is about to drip down again, a tiny bit of weather.

Business, Real Estate, hmmm, Automotive, Sports. I'd better check. It was a week ago, that oft-postponed Sunday, cold and raw gray. We bundled them in the latest castoffs from the shop, our kids forever five years behind the styles. And off they cheerfully went, good sportsmen, crammed into Gabe's blood red Rabbit for a day of roaring and mystification. There were more people there than I ever saw, said dazed Zephaniah. Uncle Gabe did explain all the rules to them, but Malachi admitted he could never make out who had the ball. But they thought it was funny for a while, those top-heavy bruisers slamming into each other, falling down, and of course they had great seats. And they could always tell Billy on the bench by his **24**.

I should have gone too.

Maybe Gabriel sparked some interest in Obadiah, the calculations, the measuring, the timing, the pattern of it. But I could sense the promised locker-room visit was more scary than fun. Three skinny waifs wandering, in their gaudy parkas, through bright steamy corridors of huge sweaty hairy men wrapped in towels, maybe even naked ones. All Obadiah said was he was glad when they did find Billy. Hey Shadrach, Meshach! they heard through steam. And big grinning Billy — I can see him, emerging, pink, full of pride and victory. Hey guys, these are my boys! he'd say to teammates. He'd pick the kids up, two at a time.

And Gabriel would lean quietly back against a locker, savoring the happy turn of his life.

All these damn uncles butting in on you, Poppa, lately.

What do you know! There's Billy Sharp, number 24, from behind. "Boys, come see Billy in the Sports section."

▼ ▼ ▼

We're still awaiting Izzy. Visiting her parents always makes her try five outfits before she can decide. She's not like that for anywhere else, and she won't let me kid her about it.

There's Zephaniah behind me in the doorway. "Can I bring this to show Gramp and Gram?" he asks.

It's their Sarie letter. "But she's not Gramp and Gram's granddaughter," I remind him, "she's Grandmother's and Grandfather's."

"But still," he says.

"Sure, of course, I didn't mean they wouldn't be interested."

"They know she ran away too," he says. For Zephaniah, everyone should take the same care of everyone else. Why did I even question it? He's leaning against my chair arm looking at the stiff pink folds of paper, stationery of a southern aunt. He holds the letter out to me. He wants me to read it to him once again.

" 'Dear Cousins,' " I begin.

Zephaniah kneels down, elbows on chair arm, watching my lips with his eyes.

" 'Dear Cousins: I wanted to write you your own letter. At Thanksgiving I missed you. Actually I miss you a lot always. Unc Linc and Aunt Iz I'm sure told you all about what I did. It's been over a month now. I'm seeing my southern cousins, but they are not like you guys. For one thing they are older and they are really wild some of them. We go riding back roads at night with their friends. Don't tell Dad, it's sort of scary. You know what I do? I remember back when I was you guys' age and I watched that scary movie with Obadiah, remember? You were three I think. I had you squeezed in the chair with me in my lap like you were my stuffed camel. It felt like my fear was running right into you, like electricity like from a lightning bolt that struck us. So they would have to pry us apart. Probably I made you more scared but it helped me not be so scared. That's what I think about when we are out riding in the dark down here, pretending I have my cousins, all three of you there on my lap. Dad said he was coming to get me at Thanksgiving but I told him not to yet so now he says it's going to be Christmas. It's that I'm not ready to come back up there. But I don't want you thinking I forgot you. Now let me give you a good piece of major advice. Don't let the other kids make you feel like you're the oddball. That was my mistake, see. Mississippi is where I'm going to be for a while so write. I love you three.' Then she puts three hearts and X's and O's and signs 'Sarie.' "

"Did she get our cards yet?" Zephaniah asks.

"She should've."

He smiles entirely to himself, takes the pink letter back and goes to put his parka on.

"It's warm down there in the South, isn't it, now?" he asks from behind me somewhere.

"Warm and sultry, I imagine."

"Poppa, how come they make movies be so scary?"

"People like getting scared, I guess."

"I was scared over at Jumbo's, you know, Poppa. That night when we heard Sarie ran away and you came back late from Uncle Gabe's."

"You didn't tell me you were scared then."

"I was scared."

"But your brothers only said the movie was stupid. We practically had to carry you back across the lawn you were already so sleepy."

"Because I tried to fall asleep instead," he says. "But I'd open my eyes, Poppa, and see these people getting buried."

"Dead people?"

"One guy got his face smooshed in. It took place in the desert. The Tomb of the Kings."

"You mean quicksand?"

"No, Poppa, it was this ancient tomb collapsing on everyone. There was only one way out."

"Wait a bit. It was a smooshed yellow face with teeth coming through the cheek?"

"I didn't keep looking. I kept closing my eyes."

"But it was Obadiah's movie!" I say. Why didn't he tell me?

"Jumbo just said it was silly. She kept making jokes. Oh yuck, gross out, she was screaming all the time. She made us a whole ton of popcorn. But Poppa, it was better than sitting over here with Uncle Doug calling and getting us all nervous."

Zephaniah has come around from behind my chair, fully suited up, but he keeps glancing back across the hall to see if Momma's ready yet.

"You mean, Poppa, it was the same scary movie from Sarie's letter?" he asks, pink paper held against the fluorescent orange jagged lightning stripes on his parka.

"It might just have been," I say.

"Uncle Doug keeps telling us about this one called The Glob. He says we've got to see it. Next time it's on TV he's going to have us over for the night. It's his favorite movie. He says we can all curl up and get scared. But why, Poppa?"

"Tell me this, Zephaniah. Haven't I at least been good about keeping the Spode story unadventurous?"

▼ ▼ ▼

"The Falcon sounds funny compared to Uncle Gabe's convertible," Malachi complains.

We're traversing the channels and lagoons that drained the ancient chartless swamps where once a lone Frenchman in a canoe meandered with his Indian guide. Every blade of prairie grass, every cattail around here paid homage to Louis the Fourteenth in those days. And we speed along concrete bridges, sweep around cloverleafs. We could be any number of places.

And here comes the strip of stop-and-go.

"What kinds of sounds?" Izzy asks after a long pause. Car talk is always slow, interrupted by the things to look at, flashing by.

"Hear that squeaky cleep-cleep-cleep? And that moogly-moogly noise underneath?" says Malachi.

Suddenly, as we pull up to a stoplight, Obadiah explodes in a frenzy. "Look, look! Look at that sign! Poppa! Look!"

Somehow the marquee on the big motel reads:

TONITE
COME CRAP
IN OUR LOUNGE

"What's it say, what's it say?" squeals Zephaniah, piling over his brothers' laps to get a view out Obadiah's window.

Izzy is blinking out at the sign. I can't believe it either.

"Come crap in our lounge," Malachi tells Zephaniah, who's seen it by now.

"Come crap in our lounge!" Obadiah pounds the back of Izzy's seat, ecstatic. "Poppa! Momma!"

Somebody must've done it in the dark. No one's been up yet on Sunday morning to tell them. But what did the letters really mean to say?

Green light.

▼   ▼   ▼

That you came in their front door and went down five steps to the living room, all glass, hanging out over the bluff, seemed like the Future to me when I was young. A high school party here, kids out scaling the crags, necking in the ravines, daredevils hanging off the balconies. No one else lived like this then, and in a house with its own name: Troutbeck. And young Isabel and younger Gabe, children upon this pattern of lake views and platforms, cantilevered, unfounded. Serious elusive little Gabriel, delicate Iz. I come through this door now and that first time always floods me.

"Gramp! Gram!" the kids are calling.

Wide open arms, loud hoots. Two potatoes are bumbling up out of their deep soft chairs both talking at once. "Oh look at you and look at you! That's my boy!" And measuring heads up to Gramp's shirt buttons and hair tousling from Gram. "Well look at you!"

Izzy and I hold back. It is always her best moment with her parents, the flush of arrival.

"Darling, and look at you in your stylish polka dots. You're coming up in the world! The Lammermoor ladies have taken to donating to your shop. Am I right?"

"Oh you and your Lammermoor ladies, Mom," I say. "Don't forget my own sister's a Lammermoor lady."

"We can't all live here in Knollslea, my dear," says wry Gram.

The boys have run to the glass wall to look at the tossing lake. It's whipped up today. I can even hear through the immense pane the whitecaps pounding in.

"No, darling, it's lovely, I'm ribbing you," says Izzy's mother, tickling at the dark blue polka dots. "Perfectly tasteful."

"My girl," Gramp says, squeezing Iz.

"Tell about the lounge, Poppa," Zephaniah whispers, having run back to the knot of us big folks.

"Let's save that," Izzy says, peeling his parka off. Here at Troutbeck they're forgetful. All we've taught them fades in the glow of Gramp and Gram. Cautious politeness when visiting my parents, coats carefully hung on coatrack, boots lined up in mud room, but not here.

"Zephaniah, you've put on a spurt, haven't you now!" Gram says. "I'm getting so as not to know you."

He tilts from toes to heels, shifts, is the awkward little boy of his grandmother's imagination. No, and she doesn't know him really at all.

Whomp go Gramp's big brown hands on the shoulders of Obadiah and Malachi. "What say, boys, about a slide down to the foaming billows?"

A grandfather's delight, his fiberglass chute, extrav-

agant beyond a child's dreams, and our boys the sole
recipients. Well, and an occasional outing of Billy Sharp's
Fresh Air kids, we've been told by Gram with a raised
eyebrow.

Gramp leads the way. "Put your parka back on, Zephaniah," Gram calls. She turns and grabs my wrist, pursing
her lips as if to contain her bliss: "It's so good for John. It's
what he's alive for, darling, I sometimes think. You've got
to come up more regularly, really you do."

Ah, there are the little lumps, the growths on the potato
skin just as Obadiah said. And a slight quiver, so the jowls,
the neck shake, wrinkly and puffy at the same time.

"Too much of our boys might do Dad in," Izzy says.

"Never!" howls her mother. "Never, Isabel, never! After
all, Gabriel's unlikely to supply us. Yours are it!" She's
fussing with the collar of Izzy's dress, peeks at the label.
"Lorraine's, what did I tell you!" she hoots. "Lorraine's no
less! I certainly have an eye!"

▼　▼　▼

Still, to this day, it feels odd, the glassy house, and these
two old people shouting about in it. They who grew up, I
know, in boxy dark rooms and peeked out heavy curtains
at a South Side street.

Gram and Izzy clinking and clacking half a staircase
below in the pantry and distant boys hollering from the
chute. I'm without function. Leave the boys to Gramp —
it's better for him — and Gram won't allow me in the
kitchen and that's final!

The so-called powder room. It whirs when I close the
door.

Taking a breather in here during eighth-grade parties,

when I was already Isabel's and almost acted like one of the hosts. And while Scott and Peggy made out in the coat closet, Iz and I seemed married already. We were the model of Couple then. They'd all come to us. Do you think she likes me, Lincoln? Find out from Iz.

The very same wicker reserve toilet paper holder, the same shelly soap dish, and Gramp's basket of on-the-pot reading. Are you sitting on your nest egg? asks a fat cross-eyed bird in this investment brochure. This bird has a way of looking snooty and pushy, informing you in a chirpy voice that doesn't quite offend the way a human's would. And inside, the bird flaps around making a series of goggly faces illustrating the steps, one through ten, and on each page an additional egg appears in the nest until at last they all hatch and ten cross-eyed nestlings peep dollar signs while the fat bird's beaky grin produces a loud smug quack.

Yep, Gramp, all power to you.

But already back then, sometimes it was too much for me, those parties, so I'd come sit here and leaf through the stock reports to clear my head. Gramp and Gram were only my age then, or thereabouts, weren't they!

▼ ▼ ▼

"Shall we all hold hands?"

"Dad, we've had this out a hundred times."

"And Izzy, wonder of wonders, hope still springs afresh each time you all sit down to dinner with us."

"Dad, just say your grace and let's not make an issue of it."

He reaches over and chucks Izzy's chin. "My girl," he

says wistfully. Gram rests her hand on the back of Mala-chi's head, ostensibly to keep him from fidgeting but she needs that touch. We're sticking to our theoretical guns nonetheless.

"Dear Lord," says Gramp, "bless my dear sweet blind pagan offspring and grant that they shall one day open their eyes to Thee."

A hint of a grin on his face. He's enjoying his act, eyes shut, head bowed, empty hands with palms outstretched toward Isabel, toward Obadiah. We five sit looking about, heads up, elbows on table. It's important. We will not be part of this.

"They're wandering in darkness," he says, "and they're refusing to let Thy light shine in upon them. They're as stubborn as all hell and — "

"Oh John," interjects Gram.

" — and refuse even to take a peek at Thee for fear Thy truth might dazzle them. Be patient with them, dear Lord. Allow them, without their acknowledging Thee, nonethe-less to take sustenance from the fruits of Thy trees and the grain of Thy fields."

"And the hams of thy pigs," says Izzy.

"Izzy."

"Amen."

"You're funny, Gramp," says Zephaniah, fork in hand.

▼　▼　▼

I pass the mustard in its tiny silver dish from Zephaniah on one side to Obadiah on the other. Gramp catches my eye.

"It's my great regret, Lincoln," he says. "If only Gabriel

had somehow seen fit to breed, we might have found ourselves with a Christian grandchild."

"Is that the logical conclusion of Gabe's breeding, Dad?"
asks Izzy as if she wasn't looking for trouble.

"Well, when did Gabe ever refuse to have a credit card
or go off and live among Bohemians?"

Gramp's notion of un-Christian behavior. I catch Izzy's
eye.

"We live in Ardennes, Gramp," says Obadiah.

"Fine town, Obadiah, despite its preponderance of
Slavs," says his jocular Gramp.

"Every town seems to have a preponderance of something, doesn't it," Gram adds. As if to underscore the off-
handedness of the remark, she's fussing with the chain of
clear beads that suspends her bifocals from her spongy reddish neck.

Izzy, with fiery eyes across the table from me, watching
her.

"But your sister Gale certainly has settled into Lammermoor, Lincoln," Gram adds further, as if I'll assuredly
sympathize with her social discomfort. "She seems quite
comfortable with her minority status there."

"Perhaps she wants her kids to get asked to a lot of lavish
parties when their little friends turn thirteen," says Izzy.

The battle is on. We've held it off longer than usual.

"Why, Momma?" asks Malachi.

"Well, I can't say I disapprove of puberty rites," says
Gramp. "What say, Isabella, we throw Obadiah a bar mitz-
vah! He's already got the requisite Hebrew name."

"I do too," says Malachi.

"But what is Gramp talking about, Poppa?" Obadiah
wants to know.

"Please, John," warns Gram, who started it all.

I find myself staring out past Izzy through the glass to the expanse of surging blue. The lake so high recently, and even perched up here I can sense the volume of all that extra water, two feet, three feet more of it than usual, spread over such a vastness. A thought of Zephaniah's old terror: the seiche.

"And what would you say if I revealed," Gramp goes on, jowls flushing with inspiration, "that when they were just little tykes and you thought I was taking them to the Brookfield Zoo one Sunday, Isabella, I was actually conspiring to have those boys secretly christened, all three of them, with Gabriel of course and the Doug Traces as godparents. And you never suspected a thing."

"Very amusing, Dad," says Izzy.

"But how do you know it isn't so? Were you there? You who refuse to hold hands with your own parents for the blessing! Perhaps you have a cell of underground Christians in your very midst."

"What's Gramp talking about?" asks Zephaniah.

"Blah-de-blah-blah-blah," says Izzy, forking a mustardy sliver of ham.

Our boys perk up when she gets going with Gramp and Gram.

"Snork-snork-snork." Malachi is being a rooting pig as he carves up his second helping.

"Darling," Gram says, "you know I wasn't saying it's religion that makes Lammermoor what it is. Plenty of Christians have that sort of taste too. It's a particular slice of society, that's all. Am I right? At least out in your backwatery Ardennes — "

"Where no one has any taste of any sort!" snorts Izzy.

"You're the one that said it, darling." A pause to enjoy her small triumph, then generously: "Look at that lake! Isn't it spectacular today! John?"

Obadiah leans across my tummy to explain to his littlest brother: "See, Gramp thinks only slobs would live in a town like Ardennes. That's what Momma's so mad about."

▼   ▼   ▼

"Remember the old days, kids?"

By kids Gramp means Izzy and me, not our own.

"Remember the days when you two were on the loose down in Chicago? I kept getting up on my high horse. I even tracked you to your lair to make sure my girl here wasn't falling in with communist agitators. Those were the old days, weren't they! We all have our old days. It turns out yours were about as harmless as mine, son. Mine before the war, I mean. I hated my president too. Franklin Doublecross Roooosevelt. Yes, I remember you in your sockless loafers, threadbare sports jacket and jeans. I'm talking about way back, Lincoln, at the start, your serious left-wing phase, before the headband and beaded belt. And my Isabella in her peasant dress."

Gram is spooning out the lime fluff, trying to preoccupy the boys.

"I do remember," I say, giving him my best smile.

"You've said it yourself, Isabella," he goes on, turning to his real quarry — his lifelong pursuit, I sometimes think — his daughter, who still won't let him quite relax with her. "That now the world is perched on the edge of something much much worse than it was then," he explains. "That we were all rather naive in our various old days — you, me, our adversaries, all of us."

"Our ideas of much much worse aren't quite the same, Dad," says Izzy. "I wouldn't object to a stock market collapse the way you might."

"Lord, I have to run panting to keep up with your apocalyptic thinking, darling!" And he is looking, for him, a bit bedraggled saying it.

There's no stopping Isabella once she gets back on that old battle line: "Dad, have you counted your nest eggs lately?"

"Our daughter keeps challenging me, Sue!"

▼ ▼ ▼

Clean plates. Three slumping boys. One argument too many.

"Let's call a truce. I have a modest proposal," says Gramp.

"It better be a good one, John," Gram says.

He pretends to whisper, so the boys won't hear, and they naturally perk up out of their stuffed stupors precisely the way he wants them to: "Lincoln, I'm going to get your boys here a PC. I know you're not likely to do it yourselves — "

"It's for their studies," says Gram in a hurry to override our resistance. "It helps them so much in school these days," she says all nodding, blinking.

"What's a PC?" asks Zephaniah. I rest my arm across his squirming shoulders.

"Something you'd have no possible use for," says Izzy. "Gramp is just teasing your Poppa and me."

But Gramp is rubbing at his eyes. A deep wheezy breath. He hadn't foreseen this resistance, or so he pretends. "I'm quite serious, darling."

"Don't push it, Dad," warns Izzy.

"Ssh, John, maybe they already have their own plan for Christmas, you know — "

"What!" "What!" The kids are squirming in their seats. We've sat too long.

"Boys, here it is. I'm going over their parents' heads, Sue. I'm getting you, for your very own sole use, not for your obsolete momma and poppa — they're not even allowed to touch it — your very own personal — hmmm — computer!"

Faces fall.

"But what for?" Malachi asks. "We have to use those things at school."

I see Obadiah is keeping his thinking to himself. I find myself looking over at him closely, to detect something. Does he feel this is some test of him, some wrestle with a demon? Does he want to know what I want him to say? Or no, does he desperately want one, for his plans, for his lists, his secret notebooks, for —

"You don't need to get us a computer, Gramp," he says. In his face a look of the adult, at this angle. I haven't seen it there before. An emerging cheekbone? Something strong, something vulnerable. "There's lots of other things we'd like better," he says.

"But it's for your studies," says Gram. "To help you practice at home, get ahead of the class."

"You know what I'd really like more actually," says nervously paling Obadiah. No, he seems very young, very afraid to say what he wants to say, but he's going to say it anyway, I can tell. He knows his chance.

"But what?" Gramp asks him, thinking: So how can I

do more for you, my little pagan, how can I win you, and even maybe how can I rescue you? I see it in every deep line of his forehead, his outstretched knotty fingers.

"A rifle," says Obadiah. "For targets I mean."

The surprise of an unlooked-for triumph on Gramp's blistered lips. More than he could have dreamed.

My son?

3

BEHIND US THE bleached and bespangled woman is lugging in another chair. I grab it by the legs, pilot it through the door. Mrs. Schnell has swiveled, pointed Izzy to the chair opposite her before I've even said hello. "Anything else, Sherryl?" says the woman. A shake of tight black curls, and all I catch are the woman's bright nails on the outer knob as the door sweeps closed, Mrs. Schnell's winter coat, scarf, sweater piled up on its one hook. The pale yellow room is crammed with us in our puffy parkas. Izzy unzips and wriggles out of hers.

"And hello, Lincoln," says our adversary. She's looking right into me, brilliant eyes. It's hot in this building. I haven't felt as hot in months.

"Hello, Sherryl. Well, here we are," I say to fill the pause.

"You'd be more comfortable — " she begins, but I'm already up and shedding my forest green shell. As soon as their down gets matted, the North Shore people give up on these, where a simple wash and fluff dry turns them good as new.

"Winter's definitely on its way," says cheery Mrs. Schnell. She can't possibly relax us with her chitchat.

"I'd say it's here," says Izzy.

"I guess you're right, it's here," Mrs. Schnell concedes. I feel it's her last concession. There's hardness in her eyes this time. It's first thing Friday morning, and she's not going to let another evasive week get past her.

"I didn't ask you both in," she says, swiveling slightly away from us toward the wall of slathered yellow blocks, "to point any fingers. Finger-pointing's up to the principal's office anyway. I simply want to update you on my concerns. All right?"

We are silent. Izzy's looking sour. I don't know what my face looks like.

"I've done a lot of talking with your Malachi the past month as you know," Sherryl says. "Two things have come clear. On one hand, he's a delightful youngster, loves to fantasize. Makes up elaborate stories to try to bamboozle me, and I play right along. It's harmless in itself, but it's increased my worries. Something's under there. I think I've seen it. A lot of fury and rage, but his cleverness nearly manages to conceal it entirely. Other boys his age are nowhere near his level of sophistication. Their explosiveness is right out there. But Malachi Trace, well, he's ingenious at turning it inside out into a kind of victimizing of himself. In fantasy, you follow? He'll imagine his own head thrust into a burning furnace, for instance. Or his older brother hunting him down with a gun through some mysterious secret passageway. You've heard any of this? Remember, Lincoln, what I mentioned when I first spoke to you, how he lets himself get caught in pom-pom, how he stands up like a martyr to the rain of balls in bombardment. His thing about endangered species, for instance. I'd even go so far as to wonder if his rearranging the letters of his name doesn't represent some desire for obliteration, for loss of self, his own disappearance."

"Fascinating," says Izzy. She's trying her ironical approach.

Sherryl looks at her as if to say, Hold your fire a second, and the light out there behind the glass bricks snaps off. Someone has just left that office. It seems cold in here now, like a cell.

Izzy stares back. She will not give off even a hint of friendliness. She loathes this woman. Why should I feel the least whit sorry for Sherryl Schnell? She's trying to do her job in this busy world. I have to be somewhat grateful she's taken so much time over our boy. She's not really as hard as her stare. It's a method she's picked up, because she's nervous. And now she turns to her folder for a peek. Why, having Izzy with me, am I not as suspicious as before?

"Oh, and the bedtime stories," she says. "I'm sure, Lincoln, you don't want to take credit for what your son tells me you put his younger brother through every night." She pulls out a sheet of blue paper. A transcript. "May I? Quote: See, Zephaniah can never get to sleep anymore because of the scary story. That's what Poppa does every night before bed. He makes it up. It's about our dog, remember, the one who bites the neighbors? It's all about how Spot — is that it? Surely that's not it."

"Spode," I say, "like the china."

"Spode? How Spode gets possessed by the devil and attacks people. Every time it ends with blood and guts dripping out from Spode's jaws, and Zephaniah has to hide under the blanket."

Izzy's laughing. She's pretending to find it all funnier than she really thinks it is.

"And then when Poppa leaves, Zephaniah has me come over and let him hug my old stuffed dodo till he feels safe again. Unquote."

"Thank you, Sherryl," I say, "for not giving credence to that particular little invention."

"All right now," she says, leaning forward toward me, elbows on her wool skirt, as if to ignore the smirking Izzy. Close up, her face is quite lovely, a quivering pulse right there underneath her pale skin. "So you're wondering," she says, "why to me an overactive imagination seems more like compulsive lying. It's because this lying, Lincoln, is what I'd want you to see as only a symptom of something more troubling."

"Oh hell, why don't you just laugh along with him!" exclaims Izzy. "He's having a ball with you. The more earnest you are, the funnier he finds it."

Sherryl has turned, leaned back, inviting an onslaught.

"He's having a ball," Izzy says again but all humor gone from her voice. She's so tired of this, and she wants me to help her more. Why don't I butt in with something definite?

"Sherryl — " I begin.

"Let me take a different approach then," Sherryl says.

The neighboring office light flashes on again. A gray shape is rummaging around in there, file drawers slamming.

"Some clever child," she says, "has been making a rather unusual use of art period. He — or I should be fair and add she, since I'm not pointing fingers — has taken a stack of red construction paper and then pasted on big white cutout letters and then secretly, probably after dark, stuck them up on the stop signs at all the crosswalks leading to school. Our patrol boys were doing double takes. I think you'll recognize a familiar touch: POST, POTS, TOPS, SPOT. The fact is, it's a criminal offense to deface traffic signs, Isabel."

"Oh pooh," says Izzy.

"Why didn't the art teacher stop him?" I ask, my heart going hollow.

"It was a free period," Sherryl says, quite calm. "I think most of the class was out doing the mural project for Christmas."

"Don't say 'him,' Linc. This is only circumstantial evidence!" Izzy says. But how worried is she? She looks so fierce, my own Iz.

"Lincoln, I ask you, please!" says poor Sherryl.

"Oh just take the damn signs down! Who gives a shit!" says Izzy out of all patience.

Sherryl grants her a calm smile. "I know, Isabel, it seems petty. But you'll understand we try to see things from pranks all the way up to vandalism along a continuum. A fire in a wastebasket isn't quite so petty. A car fire is hardly at all petty. A wastebasket, then a car. Then a house? The Ardennes Fire Department is on watch."

So now quick I'll jump in with "Sherryl, I realize we're somewhat like thorns in your side as parents go. And I'm sure you've heard about that note of ours to the principal excusing our boys from Christmas activities, but our boys — "

"Ah yes," she says, "and a certain boy wasn't required to help paint a certain mural during the time a certain pile of red construction paper seems to have disappeared."

"I grant you, Sherryl, we do things oddly," I try going on. "We're an odd family, but that's all," I say. "Our boys — "

"You see, I happen to be Jewish," Sherryl says. "And

there's not many Jewish kids in this township. But we have a nice Hanukkah program nonetheless and we have a nice Christmas program. It's cultural education. That's how it's presented. And we live and we let live."

"I will not have my kids exposed to nice cultural religion, Mrs. Schnell," says icy Isabel, "and I don't care if you have a nice Ramadan either."

"Can we agree on one thing, though? That we try to live and to let live?"

"And I suppose four little crosswalkers went splat because a car potsed when it should've stopped!"

Oh Izzy, I say inside my head, and I feel something missing here between us. If we were only on a bench together instead of in these separate chairs cushioned by our parkas. We're not approaching this the same. One last attempt: "But you called us last night, Sherryl, with something immediate on your mind, surely. You wanted us to come in first thing. Was it only these stop signs, or was it Christmas? Or to talk about Malachi's lies? Was it?"

She looks suddenly somewhat distressed. Is it a glimmer of a tear in her eye? Izzy's having her effect. "I hate to see children hurt," Sherryl says.

"Because you're afraid Malachi makes himself the victim. That's it?"

"Or other children, Lincoln. The worm finally turns maybe." She leans forward and pats my hand. She's jockeying against Iz, I can tell, but why do I let her? There's even something slightly arousing in her touch there. "Yesterday," she says, "after Thursday Sing — I wasn't planning to add this but here goes — after Thursday Sing when the fourth grade went to get their wraps — "

"What?" I ask. I can sense Izzy watching that hand on my hand.

"Well, the girls' wraps were missing. And then Ms. Wishart looked out onto the playground. Little girls' parkas were standing around like frozen statues. A ballet of little parkas, soaked in water and set up outside, frozen in place. Can you see it? Why does he hate the girls?" she's asking me.

"He!" Izzy explodes.

But, I'm thinking, of course, he wasn't in Thursday Sing either. He would've been excused from practicing the carols. And his brothers too. It's even worse. She shouldn't be singling out Malachi. Our boys would only be in this together.

"Or she," says Sherryl, cooling, thinking.

"Or they?" I suggest.

"I've had it!" says Isabella. "You just catch Malachi once in the act before you come bothering us again with your suspicions. To hell with you!"

She's up, thrusting herself into her parka, and she looks at me, fierce, immediate, requiring my allegiance.

"Izzy."

"Well?"

So I'm putting on my parka too.

"I didn't want to add that part in. I thought the rest would be enough to — " Sherryl's not sitting anymore either and she's being more herself to us now. She's so much shorter standing up. "Well, a family needs to see itself from outside, doesn't it, sometimes?" she's saying. "That's why I'm here. We're talking about a little kid. Maybe he's not in trouble at all. I hope he's not. I'm trying to let you know, so in case he is you can help. Or if you knew what might be wrong — "

"But why, Sherryl," I ask, actually putting my hand on her shoulder a second to steady her, or me, "why don't you talk to Obadiah and Zephaniah too? You'll understand them better all together. You'll see what I mean about our boys."

"They're supposed to be referred to me by their homeroom teachers," she says, "but perhaps with your — "

"We don't want her talking to our kids at all, Lincoln!" says Izzy. "Come on."

I want to tell her we can't leave it at this. We'll never sleep tonight.

"You know what, Mrs. Schnell," says Izzy, hand on doorknob, and I feel that shadow in the outer office is still there, ears pricked.

"Just Sherryl, please."

"You know what, Sherryl," says Izzy, all zipped up again, "there's no such thing as seeing a family from the outside. You can't possibly know us, you and your nosy bunch of teachers. Don't you imagine families are more complicated than that? Try living with us night and day. All you have is your clever formulas to apply. Suppressed rage! You take it on yourself to determine that our boys have had their normal urges squelched and here you come, all earnest and selflessly concerned, to unsquelch them. As if we all had a standard dose of rage from birth. But our boys aren't standard and we don't want them to be standard and nothing you can do will make them standard or average or normal or make us think they should be!"

The knob is turning. Izzy wants me to follow her. She has said her final word, I can tell. She is not going to feel any regret when we're out in the cold parking lot heading to our old gray car.

▼ ▼ ▼

"This was a good idea, Linc," she says, pouring from the glass coffeepot with its plunger, a contraption we've never encountered before. We seldom go out just the two of us, and here we are up in Lammermoor, no less. To take a day off and let Roland put some crank version of my message on the door for my one or two possible visitors. No Old Spam Today, Sorry Folks! Something. But I had to stay with Izzy. We were on different sides this morning. I had to stay with her. I couldn't let her drop me at the bus, leave me to go off alone. I had to go along with her on her pickup, help her carry the stuff, and treat ourselves then to a rather expensive lunch.

Can I finally say what I haven't said yet? "But maybe it's useful, Izzy, to have someone who sees us from the outside. I mean as long as we take it for what it is."

My Isabel looks at me across the glistening tabletop in this unfamiliar place.

"Sherryl's not all that textbooky. She's from our era, Iz."

Izzy takes a long sip, eyes closed, tense lips. She knows we're going to start talking about it now. We're fed, warmed, surrounded by potted plants and quiet murmurs.

"We're not approaching this the same way, you and I."

"I've noticed," she says.

"What if it's true? Just imagine it's true for a minute, Iz."

"Don't we know our boys?" she asks, calmly setting down her cup.

"But it sounded sort of beautiful almost. A thing they might do. Not to hurt the little girls, but to make a tableau of dancing parkas. It's not that they'd want to hurt anyone, but — "

"But Lincoln, she's got it all wrong. Did you hear her say Malachi's got a thing for endangered species? It's not endangered species, it's extinct ones! Ever since Gabe gave him his dodo bird. She can't possibly know what he's about. She doesn't even listen to him. And how can she presume to have sorted out his made-up stories from what's true?"

"But if the three of them, you know, snuck those coats into the washroom and soaked them nicely and then posed them around on the playground?"

"No," says Izzy.

My wavering faith.

"But if they did, that's all I'm asking, Isabel, and if they did and we weren't able to talk to them about it and save them from the Mrs. Schnells of the world — "

"So it's Mrs. Schnell again. It was Sherryl a moment ago."

"I don't know what to call her."

I sit back in this uncomfortably slippery chair. The people lunching around us, in and out of the shiny green leaves, are not like us. They all carry hundreds of dollars of cloth and stone and metal on their bodies and pay without money. They're looking approvingly and jealously at each other, not at us at all.

"I can tell you're beginning to find her a wee bit sympathetic, Mr. Trace junior," says Isabel.

I try to look skeptical.

"But I can tell," she says.

"I don't want to stay here, Iz. Let's pay and go."

She's not listening. Thoughts must be rushing through her head because she's furious at me and hasn't decided how to start.

"We ought to go home and lie down," I say. "It was always our rule, Iz, wasn't it? If we argue and can't touch, we get feeling too far apart from each other."

"I certainly don't feel like lying down," she says.

I see it in her hands too, knuckles tensed. She was upset in the car but with indignation. She couldn't believe the guff we'd been subjected to. She'd hardly let me speak. I know, I know, I kept saying, not to let her turn it toward me.

And we still hadn't discussed it when we picked up the donations at the synagogue. We were thinking. And I was being with her, that's all, so we wouldn't feel so different. And thinking what if it comes down to me alone suspecting the boys? Is it because I'm their father not their faith-filled mother?

"But aren't you just scared?" I ask her now instead.

"Of?"

"Part of it maybe being true? The stop signs at least?"

Her voice begins, as cold as she can make it: "All right, Linc." Then pause to consider. "Tonight, at dinner, we'll tell them the stories. The stop signs. The frozen jackets. I'll see it in the blink of an eye."

"Why am I scared and you not?" I finally have to ask.

"But Sherryl went after you, didn't she? That hand on yours. Gave you a tingle, didn't it? And all her earnestness directed at you."

I do still feel that light pressure, smooth, outside me.
Right there on the back of my hand.

▼   ▼   ▼

The cold seeps in at the door seams, around the windows,
though the hot fan whirs. I've been watching her drive. She
notices, but she's keeping her eyes on the road. We're not
heading home, we're heading to the shop, piles of castoff
summer clothes all over the backseat.

When Izzy's mad, she becomes completely sure of herself. I have to remember it's a bluff. Her dad taught her
how to fight. He always told her: You should've been a
lawyer. Gabe goes along trying to follow in my footsteps,
but he's a follower, Isabella, a good company man, that's
all. You're the bluffer! Her dad's right. She will not let it
be that her boys are in trouble, and if they are then she'll
be proud of them. She's my dogmatist. Without her could
I have withstood religion and credit cards?

But if she's jealous of Sherryl's hand on mine, of my
having let her place it there, of my looking into that stare,
of my feeling even a possibility in her suspicions, of my
thinking she has Malachi's interest, our family's interest
at heart —

And even in front of the eyes of my only Isabel, I did feel
susceptible.

She pulls into the alley, up into her slot between brick
walls. Reserved for The Surprise Shop. She's out, key bunch
jangling at the steel door. I'm behind her with a pile of
stuff.

Plop and back for another load. But first, wait, I hear
shades snapping up. The backwards letters on the window.
The Will-Open-At clock, hands on noon, flipped around to

say Open to the cold old hatless man across the street in front of the Ardennes Bowl-A-Rama. A grocery bag's weighing down one side of him, his scarf's flying loosely. Ah, he's seen Izzy unlatching her door.

▼   ▼   ▼

I have waddled stiff like an old turtle the two miles across the village, home. On the corner of Greenwood at last, and the sight of that toasty bungalow of ours, and a nose pressed cold against a pane, no doubt, because he's sensed me coming. Something out of the ordinary, thinks Spode.

There's more than the usual mail under the squeaky lid. It's that season. "Yes, hello, Spode, surprise! This day's full of surprises. What're you up to? No good?"

A luxury for him, this midday pee. He's tearing around the yard, ends up against the post the new people put in for their quaint new rural-route mailbox. That house inhabited again. It sat empty a whole year, unsalable, right beyond our bedroom. The Normans? Oh, The Norman's. Some people's idea of punctuation.

"Come back in here, Spode."

Out of my shell, and the chair's still warm from a certain fur. Thank you, pup. Oh cripe, here's Ed's annual poop-sheet. I'd better get me a glass of wine for this.

The Family Post   *Issue No. IX*

Chris did our new logo. We figured we needed a fresh look to go along with the Post family's latest addition — don't panic, not another birth announcement; we're stopping at four, right, Gale? — no, it's our very own family computer! Pat and Les have already mastered it and Chris is coming along fast. So far Marty only watches and gurgles. But look what we can do now:

Merry Christmas
to Linc, Iz, Obe, Mal and Zeph!

How's that for the personal touch? Just like those chummy letters you get from your favorite charity, right? At the rate we're going, we may have to register as a charity ourselves. But luckily, it's been a banner year for Ed. Area property values are really taking off. Ed's come in first in the office four months running. And speaking of races, Pat, our new superstar out on the track, is going to Springfield for the state indoor meet in January, a high honor. Les's big project this past summer was a giant vegetable patch. We Posts dined on homegrown produce well into November. Marty is taking to day care like the perfect 80's child, and art is still Chris's favorite period in kindergarten. Give Chris a pad and a box of crayons and look out, Jackson Pollock! Which is a convenient segue into Gale's latest coup at the Gallery: coordinating a show of North Shore graphic artists which was the cultural highlight of the fall. See *Tribune* November 11 for rave coverage! So what else is new? Well, Chris is still accident-prone as ever — chipped tooth, bloody lip, hand in car door, you name it. And Pat keeps the house crawling with third graders every afternoon but still managed to capture first prize for an illustrated science report on orangutans. Les, the quiet one, is taking after-school karate, in first grade! But, we confess, it's Marty who keeps us all hopping. The three olders are some kinda diaperers by now! Last year about this time we were looking forward to a week on the Fox River with all the Posts converging from far and near. So that makes this a Trace year. Too bad Gale's brother Doug will be off with cousin Sarie in the sunny South for the holidays. So it'll be up to us and the Lincoln Trace Tribe to gather by the Yule Log over in Knollslea with Gale's folks. Here's wishing you and your whole family a warm and peaceful Holiday Season!

> Ed and Gale
> Pat, Les, Chris and Marty

Penciled in: Happy Four-Days-After-the-Solstice! Is that acceptable? Love, all us POSTS!

POST. POTS. OPTS? Yes, OPTS. They missed OPTS. Oh Izzy, come home soon. I can't do anything but wait for you.

▼   ▼   ▼

Dark so early now. The darkest day's not far. I just caught their shadows passing under the streetlamp by the T — wiczes'. And now here they are, in a fierce gust, unwrapping, stomping. There's no sign of trouble in their eyes.

"Hi, Poppa!" "Hi, Poppa!"

This time I'm definite about a hug and kiss from each. So, it seems, is Spode. He's caught my apprehension. Am I going to keep from asking them till Izzy comes home?

"You know that kid who was crucifying worms I told you about?" says Malachi right off. "Well, all the kids were sitting there in Friday assembly and the teachers were up front making announcements, and the curtain opens and there's that kid, on the cross from the Christmas program, like he's hanging there, like this, Poppa! Look!"

"It was a riot," says Obadiah.

"They had to dismiss assembly, Poppa, and Miss Licata got red screaming at everybody."

"Third graders weren't there," says Zephaniah, disappointed. "It was our multiplication test."

"They never found which kid it was who opened the

curtain for him," Obadiah explains. "But they caught the kid on the cross of course — Brad Tokarsky."

Despite myself I say: "That reminds me, did you guys hear anything yesterday about someone freezing girls' jackets or something like that?" And then I have to think of a quick lie to explain: "Mrs. Etherege was telling me something in her driveway about a rumor her kids heard at the junior high."

"You mean when all the girls had to stay after?" Malachi asks.

"We don't hear much from other kids, Poppa," says Obadiah.

"Something was going on, Obadiah, I thought so!" Malachi tells him intently.

"Well, we just came home," Obadiah says.

"We always do, Poppa," says Malachi. "You know us."

They're putting on their work overalls, from the closet, having neatly stowed parkas and boots and gloves and scarves.

"So what do you kids do these days when the others are having their Christmas program rehearsals or whatever?"

"Go and read," says Malachi.

"Do something in the art room," says Obadiah.

"I take a nap sometimes," Zephaniah says, "or I think about the journeys of Spode. They're getting so lost trying to find Chicago, aren't they, Poppa? And they never went to a real city before. They don't know what one is."

"Poppa," says Malachi, following Obadiah around to the top of the basement stairs, "did you and Momma ever wish we got into trouble sometimes like normal families' kids?"

PART THREE

▼　▼　▼

1

I POP AWAKE.

In the depth of cold night, furnace keeps coming on, to keep up, indefatigable. A gust of warm air rises past my stretching arm. Mother and Father safe now from this awful end of February, down on the turquoise sea.

And all these things I've been seeing in sleep, of course they're from yesterday, our misty drive to Knollslea. I'm not going to be able to fall back asleep. That cold, ice cold bowl across the room, like the cold of the winter moon.

But just now in my moment of waking, it wasn't Knollslea as it is I saw but some future ghost of the village as it will be one day with parents long gone. A silent smooth roadbed, straight and ribbonlike, laid across a thawing swamp, mist rising off the broad miles of it. Over a bridge with no supports. No passing traffic, no signs. A sense that the old stop-and-go with its mushrooming motels had crumbled and sunk back into the floodplain. What was that dream road? Some remnant of a future automated highway? Because I wasn't precisely piloting the Falcon. It made its own way through the pervading damp.

Yesterday the cold had socked back in by the time Douglas drove them to the airport. They waved back even a bit smugly at us. But before noon, when we five moogled over in our cleepy car to say bon voyage, it's true, a brief tantalizing thaw was vaporizing the snowbanks and damp sheets rose off the low stretches, dead trees dimly black in the white mist and an oily slickness on the road. Hardly a passing car, and that stop-and-go strip all shut down, empty parking lots, not a warm glow behind any glass nor an invitation to come crap as we made our slippery way, jarring on the potholes.

I dreamt we were being allowed to go back just once more to an emptied house. Why dream these losses, these faint glimpses, when in fact it is always there, they are always there?

And our childhood is even always there, still, the same. Yesterday, somewhat early for the meal, we decided suddenly to show our boys what they'd only seen before from the car window. Out of the chilly vapors, the little wood had emerged, marking the edge of town, then there in the mist the low school building, pink brick and sprawling, and Izzy said, Stop the car, let's peek in. They knew it was where we'd gone, where we'd hardly yet known each other, she a little girl in some other classroom down the hall, I squeezed pudgily into my desk, doodling maps on the Formica and rubbing them off with a soft sweaty palm.

Could there have been that time in Momma and Poppa's lives, they must have been wondering, a time such as they three live in now? Dutifully lining up in cold corridors, echoings, shoutings, a teacher's bark. The long rows in assembly, hands folded in laps. Lonesome cautiousness every minute of those long days, for us too.

There we were, pressing our five sniffling noses to the cold windowpanes, barely a glimpse inside that quiet Sunday shell of a noisy building. The music room. A circle of squat plastic chairs rounded to fit little bottoms. Was it here, Izzy? Can you remember? No, first out there on that soggy playing field, somewhere out there, where I first saw your eyes. And your eyes, she said. We'd each looked at the other as some odd fellow creature, alone in a howling, hurling game. And we'd escaped to the woods and crouched and held on, wished no boy with a Confederate flag sewn on his cap brim would find us or make us come out of hiding.

How I'd keep thinking, crouching there, of what my father had shown me of his antebellum research, his obsession, tracing back the deed to our house and reading old diaries from the archive of the public library, transcribing those faint scrawls all evening at his wide desk in the back living room. Don't bother him. But occasionally a summons to look at this, Lincoln. It was a floor plan sketched on the back of a faded page, barely visible, and what appeared to be a secret room, he said. It's the very attic where you now live, and you know what this is, don't you? Pointing at a thin rectangle, one leg of the crawl space, with no indication of an entrance. A station, Lincoln. This house was a station on the Underground Railroad. He was sure of it.

And at night, in my own bed under my old map of the world, under Transjordan, under the Dutch East Indies, lying along that same doorless wall, I'd press myself in flannel pajamas against the faded wallpaper. To imagine across a century the runaway slave hiding there. I'd talk to him. Tell him I'd defend him with my life. I was going

to take up riflery. On cold nights he'd come out and talk
to me, sit on the end of my bed wrapped in the extra quilt,
tell tales of travels by night on rivers, hiding in reeds by
day, waiting. From station to station, across Illinois, across
swamps leaving no trace.

Can you see in, Zephaniah? Rub a clear place on the
glass. And this was fourth grade, I think. That's an ovi-
positor, said Malachi, pointing across the dim room to a
diagram chalked on the board. Did they have those same
desks, Momma? Obadiah wanted to know. You fit in them?
He was imagining his miniature Momma in that very
room.

Zephaniah and I strolled down along the building, leaving two clear stripes with our palms on the windows. And
soon we were all back in the car, shivering the chill out of
us, passing each deserted street crossing where I'd stood
guard, patrol boy with my white belt and shoulder strap,
hoping no Confederate hat would come along and pound
me. I'd hold out my patient arms, silently, while whispering
girls shifted from foot to foot behind me.

Malachi and Obadiah were pressing their noses to the
side windows, fogging them up, then wiping fresh peep-
holes. Zephaniah switched from side to side for a look. If
life had gone on differently, you might have lived here too,
I told them. You might have walked to school along these
smooth sidewalks.

I looked in the rearview mirror at them, imagined them
soon too large for that backseat, their three sets of shoulders, bone to bone, no room to wriggle.

We ascended the barely discernible secondary continental divide to my childhood home.

That rushing sound isn't the furnace, it's Doug on the living room couch. Waves of distant snores. He was ready to pass out as soon as he came in last night. Out all evening at one of those lounges he goes to, looking for someone from a different life. It's not helping him.

Just until Sarie comes home, he said, steadying himself in the doorway, then I won't have to go there anymore. She'll come home in the spring, he said. She promised on the phone she'd come to me not Lauren. And next year I'll send her to private school for a fresh start. Lauren said yes. Doug thinks it's because he went down at Christmas and made friends again and Lauren hasn't gone yet and won't now — she's getting less forgiving as the months pass.

I didn't tell him about the boys' latest letter. Dear Cousins, as usual. It's my dad I'm going to live with now not my mom. I hope you three never have to make a choice like that. I still want to see my mom like every weekend but I do homework better when I'm with my dad because it's more boring there. I'm going to be different when I come back. I'm sorry now I made you think it was better to not like school and try to get out of everything. My cousins down here call me bookworm, for always reading. You know what I like best? Trilogies, you can really get into them. That's all I ever want to do anymore is lie on my bed and read these trilogies about dragons and sorcery, you know? I just want my cousins to leave me alone. All these kids here ever want to do is screw. You're probably too young to understand. I feel like I could be a nun though. My mom was always dating. Sometimes I can't stand thinking about her. I thought it was going to be only the two of us. But my dad at least he sits around at home with me always. He is a bookworm too. And we always go out to movies and restaurants. I think probably my dad needs me more. When you get older it is your parents that need you instead of the other way round. Believe me! And then all her X's and O's.

Sarie, their wise teacher. What does she make them think of us? Now at the gray beginning of another morning it's clear to me for the first time: they must've stopped taking us only as we are. Momma and Poppa, not simple truths after all. But I think Momma's mad at Poppa lately, Obadiah might say. It's been different ever since Christmas, Malachi would add. And Zephaniah: Poppa looks at me funny sometimes. Does he trust us? Obadiah wonders. We can depend on Poppa, says worried Malachi. Do you think so, though? But Poppa loves us, says Zephaniah. And Poppa loves Momma. Always. But I'm nervous somehow, Malachi admits. They sit in the dark of their tunnel, shovels across their knees. That's why we're down here, Obadiah explains to his brothers. We can always come here whatever happens. Or we can dig ourselves out. Do you think Momma and Poppa will ever get married? Zephaniah wants to know.

And yet here we are, constant, familiar, giving off the scents we would recognize in any darkness, having these blurry thoughts we can never retell because they have passed across our idling minds and disappeared with waking. In all my imaginings, it's never Isabel who changes — the world around us but not inside us, not between us. Our boys, the kernel of our all-absorbedness? We have encased them. They hide inside our lives, and wait.

Because we found each other so young? Because we were both afraid? It has always been instead of everything else, this attachment. When I'm half awake, like this, I don't imagine us allowing for any other course. I will die when she does.

Have we only had some brief reprieve? We have taken this new year as simply the old one beginning yet again. Because no fire drill was set off during the Nativity tableau? Because we have heard nothing more from Mrs. Schnell? Because Gramp gave neither rifle nor computer but three plastic panty-hose eggs containing curls of cold cash. And Isabel has forgotten my doubts.

Her eyes open and close. Has she seen me in this faint light? I keep staring. Now they're open. A smile recognizes me.

"It's the same old Lincoln, for the six thousand six hundred and sixty-sixth time."

"So it is," she says.

"I wonder if that's the actual count."

"What are we aiming for?" she asks.

"Some horrifying sum. Two dozen thousand mornings of this very same moment."

"And before I ever slept with you," she says, "those adolescent days in our separate houses, I still woke up imagining you. Eight, nine or, what, ten years of pretending you, Lincoln."

Her hand has slipped across me, a gentle tickle up under my pajama top. Then down.

"But of course, with a full bladder, what did you expect to find?"

This is our most likely time. It can happen so quickly. And with the extra pressure to pee shut off while this other function asserts itself, it feels the more tender all over.

Quick morning nakedness different from drowsy nakedness at midnight.

"And how about you?" I say, reaching across. These wonderful smooth roundnesses of my Isabel in the dawn's gray.

▼ ▼ ▼

Doug is wrestling with Zephaniah and Malachi, scattering
the morning paper across the living room floor. The sound
of paper crinkling and tearing.

"I haven't read that yet, brother!" I holler from the
kitchen. Whomp. Someone is down. Slipped on the Sports
section. "I look forward all day, Dougie, to coming home
and settling in with that paper and a nice glass of wine.
Do you hear me?"

Spode is pattering around with them, trying not to woof.

"Give me that letter!"

"No, it's secret, Uncle Doug. It's private," says Zephaniah.

"But I want to know everything about my baby!"

When I come in, Malachi is picking himself up, but Spode
is licking him wildly, trouncing him back to the floor.

"Look out, Spode's going to think we're paper-training
him again," I say, whipping out the dish towel at Doug
from safety behind the archway.

"Cut it out!" Now he's wadding up a sheet of newspaper
and firing it at me. "You can get another at the bus stop,
Lincoln."

It's a free-for-all. The two boys are wadding up paper
bombs. They're going to bombard me, all three at once.
"Obadiah!" I call. "Come down and help your poppa!"

It's a chase around through the kitchen and then trapped

from both sides by Doug coming the other way. I cling to the downspout by the kitchen door. Bom! Bom!

"Say uncle!" says Doug.

"See what happens when Izzy takes off early?" I squawk.

Spode doesn't want the game to end. He's worked up to a full bark, now that the missiles have fired and the boys are looking a little unsure.

Obadiah, grown up, comes slowly down the stairs, looking us all over, schoolbooks under his arm. He's ready to go. He glances at me, pretending for one second to be my father. He's never let himself do that before. It chills me.

Doug is sprawled on the floor now, practically filling the hallway. Zephaniah enthrones himself on Doug's tum, and Malachi sets about gathering up the wads of paper and distracting agitated Spode with them.

"Late?" I ask Obadiah.

"I'll drive them," says Doug.

"It's early," Obadiah says. Even he is getting up with the sun now. It makes this cold weather seem not so dreary and hopeless to know it must end.

"Say," says Doug, flat on his back, "where do you suppose Grandmother and Grandfather are, boys? On their boat yet?"

"It's two hours later there," says Obadiah.

"If they landed safe in the plane," Malachi says, still doubtful.

Will these boys ever go on a plane? Malachi claims he never wants to. I want to be a flightless bird, Poppa, he said once. I'll be the only one left in the world who never got off the ground. His ambition, to dream of not doing something, a reassuringly effortless possibility.

Doug is struck by something. In his typical way he laughs to himself before he'll tell us why. "Mother with her four-week supply of mysteries!" he says. "Half her suitcase, Linc!"

I'm joining him on the floor, squeezing right in, and Obadiah has settled on the bottom stair. Malachi seems to have taken up where I left off drying dishes.

"In a week neither of them will need much of anything," Doug says. "They'll have given in to sun and islands. I balked, but Gale was right. It's what they both secretly wanted, to get away from here, from us. Who wouldn't?"

I'm silently thinking of Sarie.

"It never would've occurred to them," Doug says, "to do something extravagant and a tad venturesome. Each imagined the other might regard it as indulgent. They're hermits, Linc. We grew up in an eleven-room monk's cell. Who do they ever see for friends? Aren't they happiest at their desks or reading in bed? I think it's half my own problems. No one ever gave me the idea I could get out. It's why I came plopping in here last night three sheets to the wind."

Zephaniah is looking down at his uncle from above a tucked-in chin. He doesn't quite get it.

"Nautical term, Zeph my boy," Doug says. "Say, what did I do last night, Linc? I can't remember."

"You didn't tell us, Dougie. I made you drink three glasses of water, gave you some aspirin and tucked you in."

"But didn't I see Iz even?"

"She peeked in on you on her way to the bathroom."

"That's why she skedaddled out so fast this morning!"

"She had to pick up some donations all the way up in

Lake Bluff. Doug, you always think everything's in reaction to you," I say.

"We didn't hear you at all upstairs," Obadiah puts in peacefully.

Doug has propped his elbows under him, pensive. "I'm outstaying my welcome."

Zephaniah shakes his head down at him.

"But now I know Sarie's coming I shouldn't come knocking here at all hours. I should be content."

Here comes Malachi to get his books from where he left them on the stairs and put his parka on like his brothers. Spode sits in the kitchen doorway with a dog smile on his face. Why are you all flopped in this hallway? he's wondering. This isn't what people do.

The boys are lingering. None of us makes a move to get under way.

"Maybe I'll stop going to that damn lounge. But I'd miss good old Pam the piano player. People sit around her and join in," Doug says, staring at the little rectangle of ceiling above us. "I can't sing, but I mouth along when I've had a few. Or find some dim corner and hope a nice lady will give me a smile. But that floppy-armed dame, Pam Croce, she's everybody's pal, she knows all the songs, the kind of stuff you hate, Lincoln, like our parents used to sing on long trips to embarrass you. Their era. Sometimes she does organ with her left and piano with her right, flesh waggling off her arms." From his supine position he demonstrates on the boys, Zephaniah the piano, Malachi the organ. They're ticklish.

"But why not go to some pleasant place around Northwestern, Dougie? Why go out to that dreary strip?"

"You think I want to run into colleagues? In my state?" Obadiah, slumped against the front door, seriously puzzling over this. "Do you go on dates, Uncle Doug, like Aunt Lauren does?"

"Obadiah, I haven't had a decent date out of that place once. I probably go there so I won't have dates. To convince myself how hopeless I am. What're you, in fifth grade? Which is it, sixth or seventh when everyone suddenly goes steady? My day it was seventh. Probably sixth now. Fifth?"

"Not fifth," Obadiah says.

"Wait'll next year, kid. The pressure's on. Now if I'd been like your dad here and teamed up for life right off the bat! He skipped all the torture. An old married already by eighth grade. But remember the agonies I'd put the family through later on, Linc, gearing up for one hopeless phone call after another?"

"But Uncle Doug," says Obadiah the parent, "when Sarie comes home, then you won't have to go out alone anymore."

Doug gives it serious thought, staring at his oldest nephew. Malachi is watching out the living room window now, worried they'll be late. Zephaniah, the favorite, starts tickling his uncle back.

I have no desire either to start another week.

"Linc," says Doug, twitching from tickles, "get this pest off me. Hey, we'll drive them to school then I'll take you right down to your office. How's that for paying my motel bill?"

▼ ▼ ▼

We've stopped in Roland's for a second cup of coffee, and I couldn't say no to a doughnut. Already by nine only the driest ones were left. What with the bon voyage Sunday dinner and his drunken reappearance, it's been a lot of Doug in twenty-four hours. He's running out of complaints about his life. He's gone over them enough times so even he feels it's time he switched the subject. But he has no other subject. I can see him searching for one, nodding at his coffee cup, checking out Roland's signs: Microwave 5¢ extra — No free refills — This is NOT a Waiting Room NO Bus Schedules. Roland is in one of his extreme grumps. Hardly a word to us. Roland, I'd like you to meet my brother, I said. He gave a humph and went back to cleaning his griddle.

But Doug was so happy for our parents yesterday, poring over the cruise map with Father, island by island, saint by saint, the sort of thing I'd usually do. Gale's fait accompli, but it was Doug who worked up their enthusiasm. He should've gone along. He'd be deluged with dates on one of those ships. No, but he'd stick close to Mother and Father, make sure they weren't bored. Be like a family again. And the three of them would spend their time making nasty cracks about all the vapid people onboard. They wouldn't waste their time ashore on Saint Martin or Saint Thomas in the duty-free shops. They'd pride themselves on walking up into the old quarter, Father pointing out the Dutch or Danish influence in the shabby buildings, Mother carefully smiling directly at every black face she passed, Doug snapping photos for them to remember everything by and getting them tangled in back streets despite his frantic attention to the map.

"Doug?"

"Well, I can't say much for your favorite lunch spot."

"It's livelier at noon."

And then Doug says, back to his life: "Obadiah's right. Soon I'm not going to be alone. Is having a kid enough, Linc? Maybe I should go back to sixth grade and start over."

"Good luck."

"Oh crap, I have a student at ten! Off to our desks, brother."

Tucks a dollar bill under his saucer, pats my back, and he's out the door.

▼   ▼   ▼

A woman by the faint shape in the creamy glass of my door, by the gentle taps. What? It's one of Galena's Mondays and it never occurred to me, typing up my spring catalog. But it's not yet eleven. I feel sunk suddenly. In she comes, long black winter coat over a dress pale yellow like daffodils but smelling lilac-y. "Thought I'd slip in here a minute on my way to Potts," she says.

Right away she sets herself down across the room on the low stool by the flag understock. Off come her high heels and she starts pulling at her toes inside her stockings. I tilt back in my chair, watch her from afar.

"Tired?"

"The gallery has me on the run," she says. "Now it's the April show. A bunch of egomaniacs. Is there some prize for working your buns off?" She's kneading those toes, leaning back against the cabinet. "Besides, it wasn't what I'd call relaxed with the oldsters yesterday. I always get tensed up, here, you know?" Arms cross over her chest, hands on opposite shoulders. "Ed gave me the nicest neck rub when we got home." Now rubbing absentmindedly those pale wrists in the heavy black cuffs. "You look bushed," she says.

"Me?"

Straightens up, stands. Pads along the wall of maps. "So are you taking your kids down to Mammoth Cave this spring as I suggested? Oh Linc, Ed and I had a doozy over breakfast. So what's this big thing about travel when we've got the most perfect country place in the whole world? he wants to know. The children are on his side. Can't we just go to the Fox River for spring vacation, Mommy?"

"We haven't made any plans yet ourselves," I say.

"Spring vacation, driving south to the first blossoms. I don't know why I'm so damn restless. I feel ready to scream." On my old World War I map she's tracing a route through Austria-Hungary, Serbia, Montenegro, the Ottoman Empire, dreamily, and now she pads across the warped floorboards in her stocking feet, glances over my shoulders at the catalog. "Idaho? Not much call for Idaho, I bet. Tell me something, Lincoln." Circling on past.

"What?"

"Oh anything. Talk. Your turn." She's back on the stool, begins the slow process of easing into those tight heels. "Go on."

"Well, at least no frantic phone calls from the Caribbean yet."

Galena's looking at me, eyebrows perked, not going to interrupt.

"Zephaniah's afraid they'll never make it back. Wings icing up, engine on fire. He asks worried questions."

"Lincoln, wasn't it somehow awful yesterday? There's nothing fresh in any of us anymore. The oldsters? They'd rather read. They'll cruise the islands with their heads in books."

"Galena — "

"That's right. I was wanting you to talk. I've got fifty minutes to talk coming up."

Now she's clicking across the floor to that dizzying map. Maybe it hypnotizes her to stare at the North Pole. She's not turning around, not saying a thing.

"Galena, is it because they've finally gone? You've budged them?"

Her fists go tense. I hear her voice surfacing out of the silence. ". . . wasn't me, Lincoln. I can't be made responsible for everything. Doesn't anybody else do things in this family?"

"Gale, what is it this morning?"

She turns around, arms folded under her bosom, starts pacing thoughtfully. "I don't know, Lincoln. I don't know what this doctor's doing to me. I get so riled. Sometimes I get to feeling the children and Ed have some alliance against me. They're so damn tribal! Our this, our that — they think everything's made for them. They're such Posts! That's how they see themselves. Maybe it's Marty who finally tipped the scales. Why couldn't we have stopped?"

"Galena — "

"Three would've been plenty."

"Galena — "

She pushes the catalog pages aside and sits up on the edge of my desk to stop herself from moving, to make us talk face to face.

"You know what Potts thinks? I mean what I think she thinks? That you have some unfathomed power over me. You, Lincoln. You're like a magician, you somehow escaped. But you managed to have Izzy from the very start, didn't you, and you have her still. Almost as a kind of reproach to me. She says I should come right out and ask you, why you and Iz didn't ever get married. She thinks that's at the base of it. For me, I mean. Oh I know what you've said, but I mean deeper than that. So. Now I've asked. All right?" She stares down at me, nestled in her high black collar.

"Well, we couldn't get married when we were eleven, could we? That's when we might've liked to." I watch her eyebrows for a frown. "So why then later at twenty-one, or thirty-one? We wanted it to be what it always was. It certainly had nothing to do with you, or Doug, or Mother and Father. What do you mean, reproach?"

"Oh yes it did," she says, still staring down, forehead darkening, "oh yes, you two just carefully sidestepped the welter of life, didn't you! But who ever heard of a couple staying faithful for thirty years from age eleven! It's preposterous!"

"Listen — "

"But it shouldn't even be possible! It's some prepubescent idea of romance. Potts says. And over these last thirty years in particular! Have you noticed what's happened in the world? God, those dutiful soft-spoken little boys of yours must be ticking time bombs!"

I pull the paper I was typing out of the typewriter, stand up, pull back the Kaiser's flag and look across the mucky drainage ditch at the warehouse over there. It's a tingling bright winter day, every brick sharp.

"I thought you wanted me to do the talking, Gale."

"What good is wanting that? You know, back then I thought it was so exciting, you and Izzy, the way you came down here to Chicago, my big free anarchic brother. And

I wouldn't tell Mother a thing when you'd call and ask to talk to just me. But still it seemed sort of odd, you'd always been quiet types, you and Izzy, it used to embarrass me with my friends, your being so stodgy. And that's what it turned out to be again after all, the two of you slumping around slummy neighborhoods, so stubborn about not living like us anymore. You're cranks. But you'd always been cranks. That's what it is. When we were little you were already a crank, Lincoln. And Izzy was your fellow crank. Right?"

She came here to start this. She woke up with it, after yesterday, watching her kids with ours, after sensing Izzy and me being careful, separate, leaving her behind us, her and Doug too. Or letting them pass us by. Stare out this smudgy window. Patches of gray snow, icicles dripping off that warehouse, paper blowing in the vacant lot.

"I've tried to explain you to Potts. Her mouth dropped open. I told her how you don't believe in taking interest. Oh no, they saved up and paid cash for that house in that lost little village of theirs, no doubt chosen for its falling property values. Oh no, they don't believe in money market funds or credit cards. They collect old crap and resell it cheap. For a living! They won't take a cent from our parents. Of course they do have these three children, and children are some kind of investment, I suppose. But they're just letting inflation plow over them, they won't enter the race. Maybe they're some brand of primitive Christians, but no, I forgot, the Deity isn't allowed across their threshold in any form. Maybe they're Communists, that'd be something, wouldn't it, Doctor Potts? But then, no, they have no community as such, they're really quite isolationist. Still, I do love Lincoln. Most of the time his being a crank seems perfectly harmless. He's much pleasanter than Doug. His wife — excuse me, I mean his partner — she's a sweetie. The kids seem contented . . ."

Silence for a while.

"Look at me, Lincoln."

All right. I turn. "What will you ever have left to tell her in the coming hour, Gale?"

She's sniffling. On the edge of my desk, hands wiping at her eyes. "I know I'm sounding like Doug at his worst," she manages to say.

I'd better go to her. But my neck is shooting sharp jabs up into my head. Sit there and sniffle, Gale. No, I'll go to her. A touch on her shoulder. A wince. She looks up, blurrily.

"Did something stop you very young, Lincoln? Something I happened to escape? It must have stopped Izzy too. But what could it have been? Once you found each other, that was it, wasn't it. I don't really think you meant it as a reproach. Is it really just another form of love? So why do I seem to need to remake you, put you through something? For me?"

2

THE BOYS ARE upstairs bouncing on their beds. The walls don't shake, but a vibration runs through with each pounce, a pulsing of the house, alive with our boys.

I'm late for the story.

Now at the top of the stairs, I've been heard. The bedspring creakings diminish to silence, only the slightest residual tremulousness under three bottoms and three flushed faces turning to look at Poppa.

"You're all so keyed up," I say. But they'd been late home from school because of the standardized tests and we couldn't get them up from the basement till they'd done their requisite excavating. Izzy and I were in no rush for dinner. We left the kielbasa to boil and took a brief dog stroll in the light rain. There was the mirror-windowed silvery van in front of Scoper's house and, circling around, we heard the widow chatting to her poodle by an open window. Spode left his mark on every bush.

Wrapped in the extra quilt for warmth, I'm settling in beside Zephaniah, and his older brothers have flopped side by side on Malachi's bed, dodo bird cushioning

Obadiah's chin. I'm surprised. They're both expecting the story too.

"It's been a bit distressing for the three voyaging dogs," I say in my story voice. "All these complicated navigations along drainage ditches, through sluice gates, paddling suspiciously chartreuse water near industrial sites, spume and foam gushing inexplicably from rusty old pipes or bubbling up from the murky depths! And sometimes the water was almost hot to the touch when Iola let a paw dangle over the stern. At night, tied up to a drain spout, the dogs marveled at the colored lights blinking on smokestacks and high-tension lines and, in the east, a glowing sky that must mark the heart of this thing called the City. Their soppy map had long since ripped along its folds. And what good had it done them? They only found themselves entangled further in the maze of waterways, the veins of this reclaimed swampland. By now they could look back on quite a series of adventures — that Encounter with the Oppossums on their Styrofoam Flotilla, the Unfortunate Occurrence by the Dam (remember that one?), or how about the Episode of the Submerged Studebaker? And now, as they drifted pensively alongside a brilliant display of pink and orange pennants and a banner that proclaimed — hmmm — SRAC DESU SBOB ELCNU as if written by a kindergartener, they observed rows of polished steel flanks gleaming down at them. Suddenly, from nowhere, a watchdog flung himself against the chain-link fencing, snarling in a language hitherto unknown to Spode. 'He's one of the City's scum,' commented Scoper. 'A brutalized creature. I suppose it's not his fault, but all the same, I despise his sort, entrapped in a robotic task, and all for a herd of automobiles! Now when I'm up in the North Woods with miles of green forest to roam, you can be sure it's a different sort of devotion to my master I demonstrate. Why, we're virtually partners up there. It's hardly the mere vandal I'm on guard against! No, it's real game, the huge furry kind, buck and moose and bear.' And he was off on one of his war stories. Iola had perfected an attentive look that allowed her to think about any number of more pleasant subjects while Scoper never detected her indifference. As for our hero, he'd long since given up all pretense of interest. He and Scoper had split cleanly along party lines, but they were good-natured about it. 'What should I expect from an armchair radical like you, Comrade Spodeski?' quipped Scoper. 'It's dogs like you,' retorted Spode, 'who claim they love the outdoors but conveniently turn their muzzles when factories spew their green bile into their beloved fishing grounds.' 'You dogs,' growled Iola the moderate, 'let's not rock this dinghy. I don't relish a bath in putrid slime.' "

"Putrid slime . . ." Zephaniah savors the phrase, cozily nuzzling closer in.

"But didn't you buy our Falcon at Uncle Bob's?" Obadiah asks from his dodo pillow. "I mean Elcnu Sbob."

"So the dogs are there behind your office!" Malachi declares.

"Could you see them, Poppa, from your window?" asks Zephaniah.

"But it's the future, it's next summer," Malachi reminds him. "Poppa couldn't have seen them yet."

"But a man with a bit of paunch could be seen," I say, "pulling back a strange red-white-and-black curtain and staring across the ragweed-filled vacant lot toward their canal. The passing of the brown fur of Voyageur Spode must have looked to him like nothing more than a brown paper bag blowing in the summer breeze. Little did Spode know he'd come so very close to his own master's place of business."

"But doesn't he smell you?" asks Zephaniah.

He's prompting, so to reassure him: "Occasionally Spode would catch a whiff redolent of Family and admit to Iola, if not to Scoper, of a sudden homesickness. He determined to find himself a post office, when they reached the heart of the City, and send greetings to his People back in Ardennes. He had to remind himself that, arduous as the journey was, it was worth the discomfort, the confusion, even the uncertainty. It was all part of his education. And, in fact, his frustrations were not to persist much longer, for by the kind of dumb luck that sometimes sets travelers on their one correct course, the dogs found their little pram entering a long tunnel of corrugated steel, rusty and echoey and dripping with coolness, and at the other end, suddenly, in one dizzying swoop, they were hurled into a much wider stream, a stream with a discernible current, a stream recognizably of water, and the warehouses and smokestacks began to give way to tidier structures, with windows and balconies and here and there a flower box. And trees crept cautiously down to the banks, and there was a playground full of children nestled in a grove and strollers and bicyclists and people, immodestly clad, sprawled on blankets out on the grass. And then, to the dogs' amazement, rising in craggy pinnacles, a wall of masonry such as they had never imagined, a kind of vertical geography utterly unknown to them — the City, it must be, it could only be, where all those midnight gleams and glimmers originated, at which, after meandering in muck all too long, the voyaging dogs could only gasp in wonder at the splendor of those industrious creatures known as People, as Masters, as — so they had been taught — Friends."

A furious pounding of our iron door knocker. Three blows of it echoing up the stairs. The wall vibrates.

▼ ▼ ▼

I see Izzy's bathrobe trailing to the door as I'm coming downstairs, her current Wharton dangling open from her hand. Not Doug back again!

The dog charges about, eager to defend us. "Dammit, Spode," Izzy snaps. He runs to look out the bedroom window so I quickly pull that door closed on him as weary Isabel unbolts the front. I watch her astonishment spread as she pulls the door open.

A small bundled shape comes into the hall, shaking off the cold rain. Untying plastic rain hat. It is short curly-headed Sherryl Schnell. Why has she tracked us to our lair? I remember I'm in my bathrobe too.

"Excuse me please. I hope you'll allow me. Mr. and Mrs. Trace, it's very serious. Please?" A question. What can we do? I swing the door closed behind her.

Silent stiff Isabel leads her into the living room. I notice the boys have shut off the light upstairs. They're listening in the dark. Ah, she's taken my blue chair, which leaves us the couch.

Spode is scratching at the bedroom door. "Leave him," says Izzy to me.

And we'd practically forgotten there was a Mrs. Schnell in this world — we'd left her back in December with Izzy's final word, staring at the closing of her door.

"As I said, it's serious. I'm sorry. I'm in sort of a state. Miss Carswell finally reached me. My husband and I'd been to a dinner over in Evanston. Some old friends. Well, that's irrelevant. But I was so up and then after her call I could only think of coming to find you, to find Malachi really. I have to ask him some questions. To reassure myself. Or ask you. You'll allow me?"

She looks still smaller in that chair and paler with those dark eyebrows and black tight curls. Is she a little beery? Odd woman, really. She's kept her raincoat on, fiddles with the rain hat on her lap. Spode has woofed once more and given up. He's on our bed, I imagine, luxuriating, where I'd like to be myself.

"Couldn't you have called instead?" Izzy asks.

"But this is so serious, Ms. Trace, or I would have."

"Peel."

"Excuse me?"

"Isabel Peel. The boys are Traces like their father. If we'd had a girl she'd have been a Peel." Izzy's fending her off.

"I beg your pardon," says Mrs. Schnell. But what's happened? "I'm sorry," she goes on. "I realize it's late. My husband said I should wait. I wouldn't have come but I was so worried. He's in bed?"

"They all just had their story," I say. "Remember the scary story I'm reported to be inflicting on them? He's peacefully off dreaming."

"I may want to ask you to wake him," she says.

"Did the school send you here or what?" says Izzy. "Can you simply walk into a family's evening?"

164 • JONATHAN STRONG

"Please," she says. But this is not one of her interview games, I can tell. "Well, I'll leave if you like, certainly."

"Better ask your questions first," Izzy says. "I'd like to know what you're here for, myself."

"In fact, Miss Carswell doesn't know I've come. I won't tell her. It's my own judgment. I'm sorry to be so intrusive." She's smoothed out her rain hat as smooth as she can. She contemplates it. Where to start? Finally: "When did Malachi get home from school today?"

"I guess they were all later than usual because of some tests," I say.

"Tests?"

"Those standardized tests," says Izzy. "For god's sake!"

"There were standardized tests this afternoon after classes," I say. "Then they walked home together. They always do."

"More anagrams on the stop signs, Mrs. Schnell?" says Izzy.

"It was the usual Monday," she says. "Tests are Wednesdays."

"But half the school had to take them, third through fifth," I explain.

"I'm afraid that was a small lie," she says, twisting a curl.

I look at Izzy beside me. Her face seems suddenly to have no shape to it. Gone loose, gray.

"Why don't I call them down?" I suggest. "You can hear it from them."

"But there's no doubt about any tests this afternoon," she says. "No, don't call them yet please. I'm not ready.

I've just been at this dinner. This hasn't all sunk in. We need to talk awhile."

"We!" says Izzy. But I can see her temple pulsing. What is coming? Her stiff smile: "Mrs. Schnell, we haven't had our evening cup of coffee. If you don't mind? Perhaps you could use one too?"

"Please, thank you," says our visitor, tense and staring.

Izzy gets up, dragging her hand across my shoulder so I'll follow. We find ourselves, dazed, in our small kitchen. Nothing we can think to say in this stolen moment? The kettle filled, the saucepan of milk, the burners — on. A tray, souvenir spoons, commemorative mugs — A Century of Progress, Minnesota Land of a Thousand Lakes — the creamer, the sugar bowl, a bowl of cookies the boys somehow didn't want for dessert. They were so edgy tonight, all three.

Izzy touches my elbow. "A lie?" She draws me into a soft hug, two of us, something shaking inside her, and whispers, "Or is she drunk?"

"It wasn't actually a lie," I whisper into her warm ear, "it's part of some project of theirs, to cover up some surprise. They know they don't have to tell us everything exactly."

But Izzy's shakier. The lie is real.

▼ ▼ ▼

Mrs. Schnell stirs and stirs, thinking, in the green light over there. Now, raising her dark eyes: "How did they seem to you this evening though? What did you pick up?"

"A little excitable," I say because Izzy isn't going to say anything. I can keep on: "They always feel these sudden changes in weather. Foggy then bright, then rain and the last bits of snow washing away."

"What in hell do you want to know for!" says Izzy.

"I'm not here to accuse them, really I'm not," Mrs. Schnell says.

"What in hell's there to accuse them of?"

She stares at us a moment longer than is comfortable. "Vandalism," she says, still staring, and then her hand is at her curls again. "Maybe I've come to help them and protect them and to ease them through something if it's necessary. Does that seem possible too? I don't know the other two yet, but I might believe in them the way I believe in Malachi," she says.

"Believe in them! But what do you imagine they've done!" says Iz. "And what's this call from the principal?" She looks at me. I'm not helping her enough. A sense of her soft bathrobe hovering near. Iz, be careful. We can't be sure now.

"But look," says Sherryl Schnell, "I'm not trying to argue. We've already argued too much. But what Miss Carswell told me happened must've been late this afternoon after the janitor left — I'm not sure I should go into details. You may be able to tell how it's upset me. Perhaps it's not very professional of me, dashing over here after a dinner party. Good old friends I hadn't seen in so long. But I feel a touch responsible, I mean for keeping on the lookout for these things and guarding against them, helping prevent — well, there's been considerable destruction at Ardennes Elementary."

"And of course it's our boys!" my Isabel blurts out.

Mrs. Schnell carefully puts her Minnesota mug on the

stack of atlases. She's trying to be definite, clear. "I'm hoping," she says, "that it wasn't your boys. And that your boys have nothing to do with it. I'd feel so guilty if in all my talks with Malachi I'd failed to do him any good but only driven him further away."

"Do him any good!"

"I'm trying to understand children's minds, Ms. Trace — I mean Peel. It's my daily work. I keep seeing such sadness and I keep seeing such rage — "

"Rage is one of her words, isn't it?" says Izzy quietly to me. She's not going to deal with this woman.

"But what Miss Carswell said happened shouldn't happen so young. I haven't seen it, but I guess it was a lot. Not only windows but equipment. Miss Carswell was in a state herself." Then with a droop in her voice she says, "Could I please speak to Malachi and his brothers?"

I wait. No, Isabel won't speak. Mrs. Schnell, jittery, folds her rain hat over once and once again. "A lot of equipment?" I finally ask.

She looks up as if far away from me. Spode sleeps on our bed, the boys, no, not asleep — listening. Do they have a thing to fear? I would protect them from anything.

"Miss Carswell was in her office, her voice was so shaky," says Mrs. Schnell far across the room. "The police had just shown her the damage. They had some ideas. She wanted my input." Her throat catches. I think a small flooding has begun in her eyes.

I imagine a tangled sort of wreckage at the school. No, at my school, our school, the music room, the chair legs twisted round each other by a giant's hands — no, it's not like that. "Some ideas?" I ask, but she doesn't seem to hear.

"It's all because Malachi has me so stumped" comes a far voice. "It makes me want to beat my head against a wall. If I've missed him!"

Izzy, silent, is getting up from the couch. She's heading toward the blue chair, but then beside it, on past, to the hall. I'm slow to get up. She's not going up to fetch them? Accuse them of their lie? Or to block the stairs? But Mrs. Schnell sits, sadness on her lips, not looking up at me, waiting, holding her tears in. I pass her, flick the switch. Izzy at the top of the stairs, bewildered. I run up to her.

The empty beds of Obadiah, of Malachi, and around the corner only tangled blankets and quilt on Zephaniah's bed.

"The window!" She stumbles back over.

But it's locked from inside. When I turn she's on her knees looking under Malachi's bed. Their bathroom — I pull back the shower curtain. Izzy's behind me now, grabbing all around me. I grab for her hands till I've caught her and turned to hold her to me. But we barely hold each other up.

Sherryl Schnell watching us down there at the foot of the stairs. We're coming, but Izzy breaks from me, skips the last step, bursts open our bedroom door. "Spode, where are they!" He shoots past. Mrs. Schnell pulls herself into a corner. Oh yes, this is the bottom biter she's heard tales of.

The dog is at the basement door. Now we're in pursuit. They could have crept down when we were in the living

room. Flick another switch. Stumbling down there —
shovels, spades, wheelbarrow loaded with clayey muck.
And the little door on the furnace is open. Three boys
wandering inside there in the flames? My discombobula-
tion.

Spode is pawing at their plywood hatch. I kick it aside.
He leaps. Isabel hovering above me, and I'm flung on my
stomach at the lip.

"Boys!"

I peer down, twist neck — a hollowness. Shapes? Shades
of the darkness. Izzy hands me their flashlight. Fumble.
Snap.

The golden beam captures them, three squeezed together and a fourth shape, the dog, deep in there. My head's
upside down. It all tilts. What is that pointing at me, glinting?

Isabel's beside me, flopped too. We're almost falling into
the hole, bending ourselves in our bathrobes, peering. Silent tableau: Obadiah's red pajamas, Malachi's white long
johns wrapped around him from behind, Zephaniah's
muddy T-shirt over knees tucked under him, and golden
fur. Where are their faces?

"What is that?" Izzy whispers, pinching my arm hard.

From behind Obadiah's pajamas another glint of silver,
and what is that on Zephaniah's knees? Only Obadiah is
aiming out at us. "Mrs. Schnell," he says in a breaking
voice, "you can't come in."

Twist elbow in this tight space and bend my wrist to
shine light back at us.

"Momma! Poppa!" cries Zephaniah. Spode leaps to lick
our blood-filled heads, to coax us. The boys, back there in

blackness, cold rubbly earth pressing in on them. Or escaping? The tunnel goes beyond. A trap will spring, a ton of earth descend and separate us.

"Come up here right now!" Isabel commands.

"Is she there?" It's Malachi's real voice. Spode bounds back in there.

"I'm too big around to come get you or I would. This isn't a game, boys," I say.

"Come up here now!" Isabel says again.

"Not if she's there," says Obadiah's voice. "Malachi doesn't want her to see him."

"You've been lying to us, Malachi," says Isabel. "You never lied to us. You said you had a test."

"We didn't want to always have to come home right after school," says Obadiah. I hear Zephaniah starting to cry.

"Is she still there?" Malachi's voice asks again.

"Is that a gun you're pointing at us?" I swing the flashlight back toward him. Now the muzzle is aimed down at the tunnel floor. It's my old rifle.

"There's no bullets," says Obadiah. "We just have them to scare her."

"Them?"

Zephaniah's gun on his lap, too heavy for him to hold up. "It's Scoper's," he says, choking on tears. "His owner took out the clip. So we could play with it."

Isabel's arm so tight around me. Dizzy, neck aching, blurs falling across my sideways eyes. Their lives without us.

"Let me talk to them," says an unfamiliar voice above us. "I'm small enough to fit in."

I find myself saying, "They have guns!"

"But no bullets. Let me."

We're unwinding ourselves, pulling back up and out, unbending.

"I suppose it's safe. Won't cave in or anything? Here, let me."

"No!" screams Obadiah.

"But call that dog out first, please. I'm a little wary of dogs."

But they might have bullets, I'm thinking. "Spode, come!" And he does, with a happy leap, frisking and woolly. Izzy's tear-streaming face gazing at me. We are letting Mrs. Schnell see our boys. What's gone out of us?

And then in her raincoat she bends, palms to basement floor, and eases herself into that hole. They must see her legs in shadow, the hem of her coat. I expect a gun to fire, the sound of it in my childhood basement, echoing from cement and brick. But down in a tunnel it would be muffled, neighbors would never hear it.

"I'm a foolhardy woman," she says, bending her short self out of our sight.

"The flashlight!" I say, reaching it down. And it's gone too.

Spode paces around us. Low murmuring voice from below. We can barely hear.

▼ ▼ ▼

We've let her have them, do something we can't do, because she isn't their mother, isn't their father. And were you going upstairs to bring them down, Iz? I asked. But she didn't know, she just suddenly had to see them. And why so quickly baffled, both of us, so easily undermined?

We've come up, gathered ourselves into one lump on the

couch. The book Izzy was reading in bed, The Glimpses of
the Moon, sits beside the coffee tray — warped blue cover,
and the blue pot, and this blue of Izzy's robe, and my blue
chair across the room in its greenish light, Spode upon it,
watching us. He knows there's something awful going on.

"You saw three guns?" she asks me.

"My eyes were blurry, from bending, from tears maybe,
from fright, I don't know."

"Do we know our own children at all?"

I can't answer. She's shivering. She needs me to revive
her.

"They never lied before," she says. "It was a lie, about
that test. It was simply a lie."

"And the guns?"

"Why have I stopped detesting this Schnell woman?"

"Izzy." I squeeze her tighter, but now some quiver of
agony pulses through her. Her body tightens and twists and
she works her way up on the couch. I turn and get my right
knee around under her so she can be surrounded by me.
She leans back against my chest. All her hair — I push my
face into it. Whispering Isabella Isabella. Spode's eyes on
us, trying to fathom this fearful aura.

Now she's looking at me upside down, tears rolling back
into her eyes. "What could they possibly have done, Lincoln?"

▼   ▼   ▼

The three boys in their pajamas are traipsing silently up
to bed. A voice like a teacher's is saying: "Tell your mother
and father good night, boys." So they do, from the stairs,
and then it says: "Now back to sleep."

Spode keeps his chin on the chair arm, peering out from under fur when Sherryl Schnell appears, her mud-smudged raincoat folded under her arm, and we hear stumbling tired footsteps rising behind her.

She notices the dog, passes cautiously over to the archway and pulls a chair in from the dining table. We've let them go up to bed without a word, as if she were about to be our teacher now. I remember this feeling, long ago.

"No, those guns weren't loaded at all," she says. "One was their poppa's, they said. Another they bought, or I should say their uncle bought for them with Christmas money."

"Which uncle?" It stops mattering as soon as I've asked.

She shrugs her shoulders. "The third was in fact borrowed," she goes on, "from some irresponsible neighbor who killed moose and bears with it. But it's old and doesn't shoot anymore is what Malachi said. I imagine you two were experiencing considerable anxiety waiting up here for me."

We find ourselves nodding, some spell upon us.

"I know how you're not generally inclined to relinquish parental control, so I appreciate your letting me step in."

"You were brave, Mrs. Schnell," I find myself saying.

"But they wouldn't answer my questions," she says.

Izzy clutches me. I find her hands and rub at them.

"All Malachi would do was ask me questions back. The littlest one mostly cried, and Obadiah — is it? — he patted and patted him and kept his own lips very tight. Malachi had his arms around Obadiah and his chin on his shoulder. They laid the guns right down. They even let me hold one, that heavy shotgun. And the flashlight was weakening. It was getting darker and darker in there. After a few minutes I could barely see them. I only heard that familiar little voice piping along. Are we in captivity? he wanted to know. He told me he learned that word on a spelling test. But in whose captivity? I asked and he didn't answer for quite a while. When I asked if they heard about what happened at school today they all just stared at me. You stayed late? I asked and they kept staring. So had they taken part in it? Had they known it was going to happen? Then Malachi said, You want us to say yes, don't you!"

"But — "

"Wait," Izzy says, her hand to my mouth. She's afloat in some trance watching that curly head, that small woman, our own age really, on that chair with her raincoat and hat on her lap.

"So I said I wanted him to tell me the story, since he likes telling stories. The little one wouldn't look at me and Obadiah kept stroking him and not letting up on those tight lips. Malachi kept looking at me with his wide eyes, so again I asked just him for the story. He said he didn't know any stories, but then he kept on talking. We were almost in complete dark and they were so sleepy. Stuffy down there. He began to seem disembodied. I began to feel he was safe. I began to feel no one could touch him or his brothers. He wanted my answers. Why don't they like what the teachers make them learn at school or the way other kids are and why don't other kids like them and why do the teachers think computers are so interesting when they only make him want to go to sleep and why don't other kids like their brothers and sisters and their parents and their families like they do? Things he never asked me in my office. Oh I don't think he was involved! I don't believe he was involved. I shouldn't have come. I should've stayed home after that phone call. Waited till morning. I'm sorry. I promise I didn't mention your boys to Miss Carswell. It was my imagination probably, my being so drawn to Malachi, my not wanting to have lost him."

She is looking at us hard. Izzy still in her trance. I feel somehow very tired too, heavier in each limb and stiffening. It's a bit dreamlike what we're hearing. Has nothing happened at all?

"And I wish I could make all our anxiety go away till morning," says that far voice, "because there's nothing more I could ask him, nothing more I could say to him. We should only be able to sleep. Sleep to get us through it."

"Good how nights follow days," I say, as if that's the last sentence I have in me.

"You've had an anxious time, you two, sitting here waiting for me, when you didn't trust me at all before or like me or want me to have anything to do with your kids. We could all three sit up late and keep talking about them if we only weren't so tired. Well, I'll leave you and you can shut it all out for now. I shouldn't have intruded on such an impulse. You'll forgive me? Sleep is best now, I suppose."

▼　▼　▼

My eyelids open and there's moonlight in the room. The dog breathes in a dark corner. Izzy has curled herself around me scrunched into the couch pillows and I'm dangling off the edge. Sherryl Schnell has been here I remember. She was talking to us and she's gone now. Things about our boys, but too sleepy in this pale dimness

                                            seeing us the first time together alone, naked, scared, small, not fleshed out yet, shivering, where? along the lake at night, on sand, snuck out, finally got ourselves to it, entirely naked the first time in darkness and lapping waves, is it early early spring? and like careless children nothing at all protecting us, my naked little self lengthening and her soft warmness, hotness even, it seems so hot and tight suddenly in the shivering dark, lights off at last inside those sheets of glass high above us, Troutbeck, parents asleep, little nosy brother asleep, village asleep, I've snuck across it, our middle of night secret plan, we're only twelve, school tomorrow, who'd suspect what we're doing? so free

                                             "School's started!" Izzy is shouting, rushing in from the bedroom. She's holding the clock before my blinking eyes. After eight! I try to sit up. I slept all wrong. "Get up, Linc, the boys are still in bed!"

Spode is a wearily stretching late sleeper this morning, so long holding in his pee.

"Izzy, where were you?"

"I was getting so squashed, I slipped back to our bed. I didn't want to wake you in the night." But no, I'm thinking, it's been since when Zephaniah was born you slept every night through with me . . . Oh, but a bad night, yes, it comes to me.

Spode trots to the back door, bursting. He doesn't know

our waiting isn't over. He thinks each day begins fresh with hope. But what dark face is that staring at us through the kitchen window? Gabriel? Spode shoots past when I open the door.

"Are they home? My boys? We were waking up and the clock radio's talking about three suspects, and then from Ardennes, and then minors, then names can't be given out, then Billy's shaking me. Then it says Ardennes Elementary. Where's Iz?" He bumps into her down the hall coming back out of our bedroom pulling a sweater over her head. Gabe grabs her emerging cheeks. His uncombed wisps, blonder from Barbuda, his almost leather brow knit in perplexity. "So Billy was saying isn't that where the Three Minor Prophets go to school? I just had to bomb right out here. Like in the old days, huh? Billy wanted to come too but there's contract meetings. Oh shit, Iz! Three suspects! Three!" She's trying to cover his mouth, tone him down a notch. "I know they're funny little kids," he's going on. "They could do about anything and it wouldn't half surprise me but not sledgehammering word processors and video equipment! You should've heard the car radio driving out here. Grammar school vandals, decline of family values. That call-in show! The outrage in these people's voices, Iz, like kids are suddenly some species to be eradicated. And the call-in guy is going yeah, but maybe it was high school dropouts, drugged-up thugs. No but everyone calling in — it's eleven-year-olds, you can't reach 'em anymore, they're out of control already by that age, what are we as a society doing to our kids! On and on. Uncle Gabe here was bananas by the time he hit Park Ridge."

"Gabe," Izzy finally says, "they're upstairs, they're safe. Still sleeping. You remember Mrs. Schnell I did the imitation of? She doesn't think they could be involved. She was over here last night."

"Questioning them?" Gabe gulps, holding Izzy's shoulders and looking back and forth, at her, and at me cramped in a corner by the downspout. "You mean they really could be the suspects?"

Izzy reaches up to his sun brown hands, closes hers over them. "Gabriel! You think your own nephews — what did the radio say about sledgehammers? And you and Billy immediately start imagining — "

"But Iz, let me say one thing for the record. In case. I mean even if they were the three, really," he's saying, "I mean whatever it is, at their age they're mendable. They might not be later. I mean maybe a trap's been sprung at the right time. Whatever happened, and you don't even know yet. This Schnell woman, she didn't actually accuse — God, what would it cost to replace a dozen computers!"

Three small figures have materialized above us on the stairs. Gabriel notices my eyes widen and twists around. Izzy's rushing up to them.

"We didn't wake up," Zephaniah explains.

"She hypnotized us I just know," says Malachi.

I'm there too with arms wrapping around at their knees while Isabel hugs shoulders. We can still hold all of them at once. They've been away so long.

Gabriel is watching. In Zephaniah's eyes I can see dread. The older boys notice their uncle. "Gramp and Gram and Grandfather and Grandmother, they've got enough money," Obadiah says to him, making a yawn. "Most kids' families aren't rich like them," he says. "That Brad Tokarsky and that Shaun Pribyl, they'd get really in trouble if they did something like that. They couldn't ever pay for it."

Izzy steps back from him. She's searching his eyes for truth hiding in there. I look up this armful of legs to three brown heads, the morning hair, the curled-up strands and flattened places.

"Maybe she hypnotized all of us," I say aloud, out of my thoughts. "They do that sometimes to make you tell the truth. Maybe we said things we don't remember and then she put us to sleep and went away. They say you never say something you really want to keep secret though, even hypnotized."

"I'm glad they got wrecked, Uncle Gabe," Malachi says. "Now we can write in our notebooks instead. I can go off in my corner and work on my words."

"But did you think we'd abandoned you?" says Izzy, still hugging them round. "You were down there so long. And when you came up you were so sleepy. We didn't know what to do. Something is wrong, boys, isn't it? Can't you tell us now? Here we are, all awake. Tell Uncle Gabe you don't ever wreck things."

Spode is scratching to come in. And now the phone is ringing. Everything at once.

Gabriel has gone to the back door for us. "Come on in, go find them, pup. Hello? Just a minute." He's holding out the receiver on its long black curlicue. We leave the boys to the dog.

Izzy presses her ear up against mine.

"Yes?"

"Mr. Trace, it's Sherryl Schnell."

"Aha."

"Well, I see none of your boys is here this morning. I'm afraid it's probably my fault. It was very unprofessional of me last night. I — well, they should be here, though, for this. Could you send them? They can pick up green passes at my office. Have them ask Mrs. Woltz. The principal's bringing the whole school together at nine-thirty. We have to process what's happened — as a community. It's going to mark these kids, and she wants to use it productively. The school's all of ours. Nothing so bad ever happened here. Jesus, just to see it! Your boys should be here. It's my fault they overslept. Are you there?"

"We're here," I say. Izzy's straining to hear the voice too.

"With them not here," it says, "some other children may get to thinking they were involved as well. The three vandals are conspicuous enough by their absence. The kids have all seen the TV reports — police and the sledgehammer in the vacant lot and the estimated losses. It's terrible for them. And with those three boys still being held by the police, at their age — "

Izzy twists the phone to her lips. "The boy who tortured the worms, isn't it! The one who got up on the cross!"

"Names aren't being given out so I can't say," says the small voice. I press my ear closer to Izzy's. "The police were questioning them separately all night. They got it out of them. And I was down in that tunnel of yours trying to solve my own mystery. I suppose the atypical case grabs me more. Suddenly your boy was all I could think of. The actual culprits never even crossed my mind last night. I suppose no one's been thinking of them enough. How could it go this far! Well, I'm as guilty as anyone. Even now I can't get Malachi out of my head. Holding that old shotgun. That was for real, wasn't it? But we have to keep talking. And aren't those frozen parkas still haunting you too? I felt we were reaching a new level of communication last night about your boys — I'm coming! — Sorry, I'm being called. It's pandemonium here. I have to help lead this assembly. Oh please send your boys. They shouldn't miss it. How else will they work it out? And if they're not here, a rumor — yes, I'm coming! Call for an appointment, won't you? Please? I feel awful myself. Shall I call?"

I leave Izzy to say our good-bye.

"We don't have to be quiet anymore?" Zephaniah asks, looking up at Obadiah, who has a slight smile on his lips. The boys have crowded Spode with them into the kitchen. A trial is somehow over.

The silhouette in dining room sunlight is watching us all. "What! What! Tell me!" Gabriel says.

"Some boys," I say slowly, "were caught by the police. Those same boys, Obadiah — Brad and Shaun? You didn't know what they were planning, did you? Oh dammit, I don't want to keep asking these questions! Izzy, let's drive them to school. This is no day off. Dammit, and yesterday they didn't want to come right home so they made up a lie about tests! As if they couldn't tell us the truth! And that damn shotgun is going back!"

"Boys, go get dressed," Izzy says.

Obadiah, Malachi, Zephaniah, heads down, staring at bare feet.

"I want to admit," says the voice from Gabe's silhouette, "before our trip I bought them that musket, Iz, in Old Town, with some of their nest egg money from Dad. Please let them keep it. It dates from the Revolution. You couldn't possibly fire it. It's meant to hang on a wall and look colonial. It's useless but it's really quite handsome. Sorry, fellas, I had to tell them — "

"Boys, go get dressed," Izzy says again.

▼ ▼ ▼

She's polishing up a covered vegetable dish, silver plate wearing through to copper. Looks up across the rags and bottles on her worktable.

"So what would you most like me to accomplish here today?" I ask. "Rearrange the heavy stuff? Wash the floor? Do something about cobwebs?"

She's thinking, looking around her crowded shop.

"Rewire those standing lamps for you?"

"Oh let's just sit," she says. "There's that whole carton of fat moldy old books to be gone through. You might find something worth reading. I saw one about Great Lakes storms and seiches and shipwrecks you'd like. There, that green one. But shouldn't you call Roland and get him to put up your No Spam Today sign?"

"Or tomorrow," I say. "Or the next day."

"That's how you're feeling too?"

▼ ▼ ▼

"And when they met an even bigger stream it seemed to go the wrong way and they had to paddle against it. They didn't know that the Chicago River is the one in all the world that flows backwards, an emptying river not a filling one. It was that species called People who turned it around — they think they can do anything! But the pinnacles of stone and glass were enticing the voyaging dogs, and finally they managed to tie up to a friendly tugboat who said he would take them all the way to the lake. 'But what's a lake?' asked Iola, who'd never been out of Ardennes before that summer. 'A Lake is a larger sort of Pond,' said Scoper. 'In the North Woods you see a lot of them. The moose and bear come down to drink and loons yodel their spooky cries from one shore to another all night long. That's what I call Real Wilderness!' But Spode said he thought this was a greater kind of lake. He barely remembered having seen it once. Hadn't his people taken him to visit a gray old pair who lived in an invisible box on a high bluff? And down below, to left and right as far as he could see, there was sand, wasn't there, and in front of it only water with nothing on the other side? 'I can't explain it to you,' said Spode. 'It wasn't water such as we understand water. It heaved and swelled all on its own, not with a current exactly but in long ridges rolling and pounding onto the dry sand. I guess I was just a pup when I saw it, so perhaps I exaggerate.' "

"No but we did take Spode there," says Zephaniah, "back when I called him Boner, remember, Poppa?"

"Go on, Poppa," says Obadiah from over there beside his brother. And Izzy in the dimness at the foot of Malachi's bed, leaning against the window frame. It's her first time for a story. After that slow silent lonesome dinner of ours, I thought maybe we could hear it all five together. Spode himself, of course, elected to remain by his favorite heating duct.

"Go on, Poppa," says Malachi.

"So the tug swept them under great iron bridges between such walls of stone that Iola must have felt she was entering the Gates of Heaven, for she solemnly took up her hymning — 'See his banners go!' And Scoper, affecting to be preoccupied with keeping the pram inside the tug's wake, couldn't conceal the awestruck expression of his black eyes. But Spode, unashamed and unburdened by thoughts of either Heaven or Hell, looked with deep philosophical curiosity through the fringe of his topknot at these wonders as they passed. 'People seem to have mastered things more than I previously imagined,' he admitted as a pure white marble palazzo came into view. It was smaller and more elegant than the highest towers but it was nevertheless most impressive. 'The Wrigley Building!' the tug informed them. And it did somehow wriggle in the shimmering summer light. But soon, with the high peaks now behind them back where the sun was beginning to drop, what was that thin line they had glimpsed ahead? What was that huge openness? Could it indeed have no end at all? Was there something even more masterful than People, rippling wet with a power of its own, something deep under these rolling ridges pounding the shoreline the dogs were just then passing? 'Come out with me!' tooted the tug. 'Let's have a good look back at the most beautiful city in the world.' A typically boosterish Windy City tug, of course, but how were our dogs to know anything to the contrary. 'Oh my poor stomach!' howled Iola, her black lips going distinctly gray as the pram crested, and plunged, crested and plunged. But it *was* beautiful! 'Just imagine how it shines at dawn,' tooted the proud tug, 'when the sun comes up out of the lake and transmutes all that glass and steel into a wall of diamonds!' Spode, however, was still looking to the east. 'But all that water!' he murmured as the pram kept rocking to and fro — bow, stern, bow, stern — cradled in the tumult of the waves.''

3

FEVERISH. Little sleep all week and yet another night of it. Isabel manages better — because for the first time in all our years she finds herself set back, and so she sleeps it off and each morning she starts a bit slower.

That day at her shop we put up the vacation sign, bolted the doors and left it behind for a while. And Wednesday when she came with me to the Northwest Side we reached the same conclusion. We're our own bosses. We have a bit of cushion. We can shut down if we like. In all our years we never have.

I'm sweating, coming down with a cold. It's the approach of spring, an atmosphere that unsettles my innards because I move more slowly than the change of air and light. If the world was on a wider orbit, had a longer day, a slower season, but instead it presses us on and we can't take our own time.

No — this fever, it's the boys. I can convince myself otherwise only for a short spell — even if they've returned the shotgun to Scoper's owners down the block and Uncle Gabe's musket's a rusty antique and my own rifle is safe now in my office wrapped up in the Kaiser's flag.

Because Sherryl Schnell somehow loves our middle son so. What was it? Drawn to him, she said. That someone else should find such fascination in him. Is it my idea of what is to come? When a girl decides — it's girls first at that age — that Malachi, that Obadiah is to be hers. When she writes his name over and over in her notebook.

Is it the fever of curiosity in me?

I search across the dark room for the rim of the bowl, faint and gray. If moonlight would strike it, a token of coolness. Isabel lies flat on her stomach, flat into the bed. I must get up and wipe my forehead, take off these sweaty pajamas. Or if I might wander naked around the dark cool house for a while?

▼ ▼ ▼

Nothing to help me sleep.

My own stories of waiting and wandering — of roasting Woofles over a campfire on the narrow sand, of canine awe at the Planetarium, where everything rises and sets and whirls — but these stories must recede quickly and when the light goes out I've left them walking in the flames of some story of their own. What faith are they keeping? They still sleep so soundly.

And tomorrow the Fresh Air kids will be making their spring journey to the luxuries of the North Shore, where they'll stand shyly goggle-eyed before Troutbeck's glass expanse. Such vistas as they have never seen in their cramped city back streets. And when they'll slide and slide and run the beach and Gram will keep her thoughts to herself for Gabriel's sake and Gramp will be in grandfather heaven or as close to it as he's likely to get with his disappointing son.

And his real grandsons will be there too. Will they romp like the others? Because they know it's Billy's day and Uncle Gabe knows they'd just as soon not but knows also that they will, because he's their uncle and it makes Billy feel good in the family.

A thought to compound feverishness — I'm sleepless at that thought. And when will we feel good in our own little family again?

I'll let them descend now through the ceiling over our bed, three sleeping forms, floating on quilts like fair-weather clouds. I'll summon them from behind my closed lids. They're still only children — I tell myself that again and again. And they have immense secrets in those small heads. No, says the voice of Obadiah, lips barely moving in sleep, we know you can't understand us, Poppa. We'll go play with those city kids and they won't understand us either when we talk. And Malachi's sleep-voice pipes in: We talk with different words, Poppa, you taught them to us. But then why don't you understand us? asks Obadiah.

Their voices don't wake sleeping Zephaniah, curled into a hedgehoggish ball on his quilted cloud. We should've told you about the stop signs, Poppa, Obadiah says in a sleepy echo. And Malachi: We'd like to make all the signs in the world different, Poppa. Old Spam. Sbob Elcnu.

I can't sleep.

But Mrs. Schnell, Poppa, says Malachi's fading voice, she wanted us to tell her everything that was wrong. Everything! You didn't make us do that, Poppa. We only wanted to tell you the good things, to make you happy. And Obadiah, floating up, his cloud condensing now against the ceiling: Why would we ever make you sad?

I open my eyelids. There is grayness.

I huddle closer to Iz. She won't wake. I can even reach around her and squeeze her to me and she'll sleep on, her dreams buried too deep in this weight of awful worry.

We're losing them.

▼   ▼   ▼

We go on as if nothing had happened. They brought me my breakfast in bed, our Saturday morning treat of pop-up waffles. And after all the rains, a bit of sun began to take the wet slick off the street so now it sounds drier out there. And I stay in bed sweating and shivering. We could all stay home today too, Izzy said, glad for an excuse. But no, we are dependable. Even if I'm bedridden, the boys mustn't fail Billy. And besides, Iz, I said, there's something they may see in those Fresh Air kids, something new to them, from a world they've never been to. Dirty words, said Isabel. That too, I said.

Activity next door at the Norman's, as I always envision their name. They're an invisible couple. Their automatic garage door opens and out slides a sleek silver loaf of a new car, like all the cars now. Where are the bathtub Nashes, the stripe-nosed Pontiacs, the holes on the flanks of the Buicks of my childhood? Where are the Kaisers and the Frazers?

Spode has been watching a shadowy shape reach out from their car window into their conveniently placed mailbox. Who writes to these Norman's?

Empty day without my own family. They're with Isabel's blood now. What do they say about me when I'm not there?

▼   ▼   ▼

So Spode will come along. There on the shelf beside the basement door, the sack of moldy forgotten potatoes. "You won't tell on me, Spode?"

I found batteries amongst the rolls of tape and string in a kitchen drawer. This torch shines before me, allowing my trespass. There below, their hatch.

"Come on."

He leaps as soon as I've slid back the plywood and he's gone into the darkness. I'm slower at lowering myself. These pajamas will get muddy, but I'll pop them in the washer as soon as I come out. Then wander naked the way I wanted to last night? Spend an hour of my feverish day naked and shivering waiting for pajamas.

But first.

Ah, there's Spode, sitting, waiting. It's awfully narrow down in there. With my torch arm outstretched I can barely slide in on my stomach. It's only one moment of tightness, like a cuff, and now it's opening a bit.

"Spode, I see you're armed!" The musket propped against the wall beside him. Where they sat facing Sherryl late into the night, where they outlasted her and never faltered. But there's another opening behind. They weren't backed into a dead end at all. "Move, Spode." A tiny cardboard sign: Come Crap In Our Lounge. But can I make it through? It drips in there. A second entrance, inner chamber. No idea they'd dug so far! "Spode, you'll fit. Go on in." But can I? Off with pajama top to slide better. Chillier in there. The light sparkling off the dog's eyes again — he's no longer dog, he's spirit.

Fever washes at my forehead, pulsing to escape. Press myself to cold mud. Calm. Still. The panting of Spode and

my own heart. No secrets here, just muck? I must go in.
If I'm caught between and plug up our air? I'm crazy.

Thoop, and I'm getting through.

Spode moves so that he may curl up beside me in this
muddy burrow and I see he's left a paw print on something
white. Open page of Obadiah's pocket notebook. Yes, it is.

if I tell him to he does it

Wait. A trespass. Snap it shut. But he's my own and I've
never before . . . What page was it open to? He left it as a
trap! If I tell him to . . . something. Of course, I can find it
by the paw print and the blame for disarranging will fall
on Spode. Spode removed the hatch all by himself, Obadiah.
I'll leave it pulled over just enough to fit a dog. They'll
scold him.

And this book I'm holding? If it was up in the light on
his desk, under his bed, no, I wouldn't read it.

DO NOT GO ON

His title page.

THIS IS NOT FOR YOU MALACHI!

One more.

POTS NOW!

Evidence. But here it begins. All in blue. I read blue words
in this golden disk from the flashlight.

YEAR ELEVEN
When Momma was ten she did not know Poppa yet. Poppa
did not know Momma either except maybe he saw her

at school. When they became eleven that is when they met they told me. Then they went out for nine whole years when they still lived with their family. Then when they became twenty that is when they decided to move in instead. They lived at 340 W. Ashwood Apartment 4. Then they lived at 326 Ridgeway Court North. That was 1968. Then they lived in one more place I forgot. Then Momma got her Surprise Shop and they moved to Park Ridge over the hairdresser salon. Then Poppa got his office. They did not have enough money and they did not borrow from their family. Uncle Gabe let them stay in his Uptown apartment when he had his Saint Louis year. Then they had to sleep on the floor of Poppa's office or sometimes at Momma's. So they did not think about kids

No, we did, Obadiah, we thought about you, exactly you. Now all surrounded in this darkness and the panting of dog.

about kids yet. Then they had enough money finally. So before I was born they moved to Ardennes where it was cheap. Into this house we still live in but our attic was not insolated yet and no upstairs bathroom. So that is the end of the ten years before kids. Then there was the ten years with kids. First me then Malachi then Zephaniah. Now it is the end of the next ten years. That means when I became ten I really started Year 11. Mrs. Ober explained it why it is the twentieth century even though it is 1985 now. Because the first century was up to 100. Then the 2nd century from 101, 2, 3, ect. So the end of the 20th century is 2000. Then 21st century starts 2001. That will be mostly my century. Poppa and Momma will be old people. Spode will be dead I'm sure. But you never know if you are going to die. I can die before I ever finish Year 11 and become officially 11. It is ok to think how I will be mostly alive in the 21st century though because I probably will be.

Obadiah you ponderer, you old soul — my fingers have frozen. Next page.

MY BROTHERS

I do not remember when my brother Malachi came. I think I remember when my other brother Zephaniah came. I was in my third year. When my brother Malachi came I was in my second year age one and two months. My Poppa took me to his office to play with flags and stay out of Momma's hair. I am very close to my Poppa and Malachi is more very close to my Momma. But we are all very close including Zephaniah. There are bad kids at school who say things about their mothers and fathers. Malachi does not know what it means yet. Mother-F, I mean. I will tell him things when he is really ready. These boys Brad and Shaun and Ivo are the ones. Malachi lets them hit him in the hall. They want a fight but he never does any thing back. It drives them bats. He never told Mrs. Schnell those things. We have our pack we made. Never tell what really happened. I hate kids going up and saying he did this and he did that. We will never tell on the bad ones. They can not afford it. Kids make up stories about us because we do not like sports and recess and go to Christmas and Hannakuh programs. I could write down all the crazy stories they make up about us. We did the

The page with the paw print!

pots signs to confuse them going to school. They will never figure out. Malachi is my loyal brother because when we have a project to do if I tell him to he does it and he never asks why. It is hard to be oldest brother. Poppa is oldest brother. Our cousin Sarie is a only child.

Then Aunt Lauren had to have a historectomy. I am lucky to be able to have a brother so close to me. I can be mean always telling him what to do but he does not mind.

WHY ARE WE BASTARDS

"Spode, stop it. You're kicking it in my face. Settle down."

WHY ARE WE BASTARDS

A bastard is a person who does not have a mother and a father that are married. Divorced does not count. Momma and Poppa did not decide to ever get married. They love each other any way. Love is not the same as being married. That is a fact but other kids say its not true. Most of the kids do not really know about the world. They go along with every thing except the bad kids. They showed their dicks on the play ground. They hate the girls. It is my fault they got the idea to freeze the girls wraps. I did not mean for them to. It was just a funny idea. What if they tell on me too. Being bastards is different then other kids. You have to work every day to be sure your mother and father are not disappointed

Obadiah, no —

            not disappointed in you. Because it is better to have a family that you have to always work at. That is what Momma beleives. Kids who do not work at things are two kinds: boring kids like Pat and Les are or bad kids like Brad and Ivo and Shaun. Jumbo and the other "eggs" are boring and dumb as my little cousins, just fat. My cousin Sarie was sort of a bad kid but not meaning to. It is better being bastards than have your parents divorced. Sarie ran away it was so lonely. We are proud being bastards even though it is our family secret. Poppa beleives how you feel inside is why you are happy. It does not matter what the world would think. He does not beleive in credit cards for that reason. He says you should pay cash. Then there's no problem. Like for our house they saved up for years and it was the cheapest house anyway. Poppa and Momma were in the newspaper back when they were 24. She has the picture in her drawrer from the Chicago Daily News where you can see Poppa and Momma running from the tear gas. We are a special family not like others families.

WORK AT IT!

Some day we are going to have our beautiful lounge. Poppa and Momma can not tell if we want to dig our escape tunnel or what. They do not ask questions. They like us to work at it keeping out of their hair. Every day we have to do our digging. It is a big project. The bad kids would never dig a tunnel. Because they would not understand what it is for. They would like it so they can sneek out at night and light a car. Ivo's big brother Jan lights cars he says. I think he lit the Baracuda on Greenwood. They want to smash things and blow up school. What good is school they say? The trouble is I agree with them. I had a dream I was helping Shaun and Brad break all the windows at Village and Mrs. Schnell thought it was Malachi. Malachi is 100% not a bad kid. I talk to the bad kids but he does not even when they hit him. Malachi beleives in one thing: you never let them see when it hurts. He said did I know how much it hurts for mothers having babies? It is the worse thing in the world. That is what Momma had to do in order to have children. Malachi's hobby is animals. He knows every thing about reproduction. But he does not know about what Ivo told me about fuck. I will tell him when he is ready for it. It is why you can have children any time. You do not have to be married. Married is not magic Momma says. Our family does not beleive in magic or god and those old supersticions. Kids would beat us up if they found out. You have to protect yourself. What if they even lit our house? That is one more reason for a tunnel. The time might come in the

21st century Poppa says. There could be no more world.
Or there could be the haves and the have nots. There
could be lots of illness from viris or from cemichals. Then
there could be war even here like in the civil war. Because
the computer litarit against the people who arent computer litarit. Some day we will be alive and Momma and
Poppa will be dead. We will really be lonely then because
who will understand us.

MY MOVIE

I saw my movie again. How did I know it was going to
be my movie? I did not reckonize it first. Jumbo then told
me the name of it. I thought it looked so familiar. This
was back on the night when Sarie ran away. It was so
scarey when I was little and that is why I decided on the
tunnel back then and always thought about it untill we
really started doing it in 1982. I was seven. At first it was
just like our indoors sand box. The man in my movie had
yellow cheeks and his yellow teeth came through. I had
to look at him now. It was not so scarey except to Zephaniah. Not really a monster movie like the Glob but
a horrer one. I did not tell them it was my movie. I was
just a little kid when I saw it. No wonder!! This is what
happened. There really was a tunnel and all the people
were getting buried. So I remembered it. That was when
I got the idea if I had a tunnel it would not be so scarey.
Like this is our house and our room and my desk and my
goose neck and my bed. Maybe the tunnel is for us to
escape but we could also get back in that way and no one
could tell. Or we can be in our house and they cant find
us. In the movie the bad people found the secret way,
though.

NEW YEARS

I am going to make the history of my family like Grandfather. This is new years day. In four months I will be 11
which means I will be in my twelfth year. Next I will
be a teenager. I will be able to buy furniture for our

lounge. We will always be best friends as brothers. If you are a forener or Asian refuggee like Quy McAllister you would stay with your family untill you became more like Americans. So that is the reason why we three stay with eachother more, we are not like Americans usually. We have Spode too. We have Momma and Poppa and our hole family. Even some of them we dont like. That is enough. Poppa does not want us to be computer litarit and religious. The reason we would rather have a gun is for protection. That is what we will use the money for. So what will be the answers to my history this year 1985: Will Sarie come home for one? What will Mrs. Schnell do against my brother? She is the one who does not leave us alone. What if she finds out I told Ivo about the frozen idea. Or when I said I thought audio visual was boring. Or when I wrote the bad word on the computer.

Blurs. These blue words swimming in fainter yellow light. Another battery going? Feverish feverish — Obadiah's thoughts racing in me. Turn the page. Oh!

Poppa thinks the world is bad. He is right. They do not try to help people. He and Momma were protestors and what did they get? The tear gas. These stories Poppa use to tell at bed time and Malachi could hear to. Zephaniah was too little so he was already asleep.

Sleeping babies, sleeping boys, every night under our one roof, back then, and my deeper sleeps then, softer worries — how this day even seemed so far off.

was already asleep. Poppa's stories were scary too. There more exciting that way. Stories have to be exciting or why would you listen. And when you pull up the covers you feel safe and cozy in there. And Poppa kisses you good night.

Must be open sky over all this dripping earth. It's not even our house above me, they've dug so far. What is up or down? These pages. Many more? Child, pondering and pondering. Where was that page with the paw?

WHY ARE WE BASTARDS

To leave it here where I found it. My awful head — Spode is scrabbling in the dark. If I could keep reading. Poppa kisses you good night? This book is your brain. I'm trespassing.

> kisses you good night. Life is more scarey to kids because they do not know more about it. Any thing could happen. Why does Poppa tell Zephaniah the Spode story? I think Momma told him to make it not as scarey. Momma is not scared of things as Poppa but she is very mad at Gram and Gramp because they are biggited. I love it when I go kiss Momma in bed before I go up to bed and she is reading and laughing over it. I want to read those fat books by Edith Warton & Sinclair Lewis when I get older. She likes books by her favorites. Poppa has more Atlasses then any one. He is a avid collector. People write him letters at work so they can trade. My parents have lots of interests. Anyway New Years is the birthday of the 20th Century. It is in its 85th year even though it is already 1985. I thought it should be then in its 86th year but Mrs. Ober explained because there was no year zero. It went from one B.C. to one A.D. So to have a century you have

This is dizzying me.

> to have a century you have to get to the end of year 100. Malachi gets mad when I explain him this.

Sons . . .

him this. I will be 100 in 2074
but I will never be 100 I am sure.

"Spode, what're you doing? Where are you?" This air. My
foot's stuck in muck. Flip one page more.

WHAT FUCK MEANS
Poppa did not tell me this. Ivo told me. I would not ask
Poppa. We learn it in May in Grade 5. We get a book called
You. They are on Miss Licata's shelf in back. "How come
you dont know what fuck means? Are you a retard?"
What Ivo said. First I did not beleive when he said it. I
know about reproduction but not this fuck stuff. If

Hollow falling thud, louder, muddy rain. What's happened?
"Spode!" Snarling, no, whining, whimpering, a tiny sound.
Scrabbles? My faint beam. Where's that hole? The tunnel,
the narrower part, no, it's come down on him. Black walls!
But he's getting out the other side. Where was the hole?
My air! It's slippery, I'm covered with mud. Here? "Spode!"
Tiny sounds? But no sound. He's out the other side. This
is not panic. I can dig out too. Soft, muddy, my flashlight's
all muddy, faint, fainting. More will come down. Don't
even breathe. What's that? Tiny sounds? Your fat ass, I
heard. Was that it? Lisa you fat ass. Above? Lisa! "Jumbo!
Jumbo!" This is not panic. For my children. "Lisa! Lisa
Etherege! By your garage!" For my children. For Isabel.
"Lisa! Under the ground! It's my voice! Mr. Trace next door!
Hear my voice up there?"

▼ ▼ ▼

They are me now. Obadiah is. I hear him. He sounds like
me. I've taught him. I hear him saying what he's said.
Sirens? And stomping up on the earth. Take no breath. All

darkness. He sounds like me. Did I mean him to go back and begin again? So feverish and slippery and the light's under mud. The earth's shifting. New underground streams, veins opening and flowing, draining. Where are the edges of this air?

▼ ▼ ▼

"We're getting to you, Mr. Trace. We got to be real careful." Young man's voice. "Fire department's coming."

"It's Lisa's mother. Hear me? We called your wife too! She's coming. She's at her folks'. We found the number by the phone."

"We don't want it starting to cave in. It's Rodney from across the street. Hear me? We'll get you out. Here's the fire truck. Can you keep talking? I can listen to exactly where you are."

"Your house was locked. We couldn't get in. Lisa was freaking. We smashed a window." Boy's voice. Extra Large.

"They're here!" Three eggs screaming.

"But the dog!" I'm yelling. Put head back. Sludge pouring into my ears. Obadiah's voice warm in there. Making a history of my family. What dog? I think I hear. The notebook! I have to leave it open at that page. He'll know. But he'll know. He already does know. Poppa who didn't trust him, had no faith, didn't understand, Poppa, who is you now anyway, who is you, Obadiah.

▼ ▼ ▼

A shaft of light, a shovel glinting. What new sky?
From this open foxhole. And a crowd of strange neigh-

borly faces waiting above us, to welcome us back. Dizziness . . .

▼   ▼   ▼

"The dogs saw it, Poppa. It was all glass like ice cubes. Can you hear me?"

"Fix the pillow, Momma," says Malachi. She does.

Then Zephaniah ahems, to tell the end of his story to me. "It had a slide coming down from it and all these kids sliding down."

"What did Spode think it was, Zephaniah?" Obadiah asks him.

Maybe I'm asleep.

" 'It's like a waterfall,' said Spode," says Zephaniah being the storyteller. " 'But for kids not water,' said Scoper . . ."

". . . Scoper being literal-minded," I add.

"What, Poppa?"

"Sshh."

Blackness.

"Spode had a funny feeling, Poppa. Maybe he saw it all before. But from up top there. Not from being out in the lake."

"He could tell by the aura," says Malachi.

"But then comes this seiche, Poppa. Remember you told us how it could happen on the lake anytime?"

"I thought you'd forgot about seiches, Zephaniah," Izzy says.

"Poppa said!"

"You got over being scared of seiches years ago, when you were five."

"Oh Momma," says Malachi. "It's only nature."

"Wait. Wait. I'm telling it. Then comes this seiche. And see, Poppa, the dogs' boat gets way up in the air on the top of the seiche suddenly and it's sliding away away away. It's up as high up as Troutbeck and all the kids can see the dogs in it. Then it's sliding back back down away and they can't see it."

"But what about all those kids!" says Obadiah.

"They all got back up top," Zephaniah explains, "before the seiche crashed. 'What's that boat with those stupid dogs doing!' they were all saying. It was going so fast away away down the other side, and it was just a tiny thing like Malachi's old bird nest floating away."

I hear sniffling.

"We didn't ever see Spode again, Poppa," says Obadiah.

"Maybe they landed over in Michigan," says Zephaniah. Do I see him squeezing onto his biggest brother?

"Or maybe they drowned," says Malachi.

"But Spode at least, boys, we didn't ever see again," Isabel says, drawing near. "And we'll always have to wonder about him, won't we?"

▼   ▼   ▼

I can only imagine it is Sunday morning and she is out in my foxhole, planting something. It's spring soon, isn't it? This fever will lift. I will not be so hot and so cold forever. She'll make her garden in all that black black earth.

4

WE HAVE MADE love several thousand times. This last a glimpse of our first, not yet twenty-nine years back. Our bodies changed slowly after the fast early change. Slight expansion of stomach, slight furring at base of spine and where chin hits chest. And in her? Nothing really — a loosening, a softening. I see in her face each of our ages. Obadiah imagines perfect processions of even hours. Not so, son. The weight of this particular hour, lying here, mulling, this midweek midnight, from which everything seems to fall down declivities into seepage, lost from view. I'm flattened beside flattened Isabel. We're spent once again.

My terrible game — no, please, don't let me, Isabel, breathe softly, stay right here.

I saw it in my fever but don't let me see it now. Still, mightn't we go with our boys a little of the way? Did I maybe even propose such a thing? Or was I in some strange ill heat?

There have been dreams. I had entered by the furnace, hadn't I? And my faint lamp urged me further in. And I had somehow seen myself three carefully counted decades ago when I was as he is. By then Mother and Father had already spoken deep into my most private brain, and the new map she gave me which wiped out Persia, Palestine, invented Pakistan West and East — it never seemed like the world. Earlier, later, any number of odd maps with slices cut out of oceans or Greenland unnaturally enlarged or Antarctica a ring round it all, mere information, hobby, clutter. I never loved but one map and Isabella, discoverer with me.

"Izzy?"

Nothing. She must have these moments when she counts her blessings too.

Whisper: "Sweet heart . . ."

How have I been allowed to hold on to everything till now?

We've earned a wedding, godless, priestless, ringless. And shouldn't it be off in the forest preserve at the burnt site of Spode's river house, maybe, those campfire ashes I claimed on our dogless Sunday meander as evidence of my tale's beginning? Yes, here it was, Zephaniah, as I told you, his foundations. Hunters, he said, they burned it down. So it would seem, I said. "After Spode and Iola and Scoper had set out on their ill-fated voyage — " No, nothing left standing. This was where the door was, said Zephaniah. This is where he peeked out at the hunters' canoe, remember, Poppa? . . . So there could be our altar.

Whom would we invite? Two sets of parents, three siblings, their mates, yes and for the boys their Aunt Lauren too. And Sarie will stand between those two lonelies, keep them safely from each other, bound through her till death. And perhaps a swarm of city kids surrounding thick Billy. And the Ed Post tribe, told to shut up for once. Galena at my side, Gabriel at Izzy's, Douglas staring up at me. Can he believe his eyes now? Don't do it, Lincoln, he whispers, desperate, just before we start. Take it from your little brother who knows! But Douglas, you always . . . I know, Linc, but that was then.

Our boys will do our marrying. Their vow: We'll always be yours. Their blessing: Poppa, Momma, you don't have to worry over us, we'll take on worry now.

John Peel Susan Hubbard Isabel Peel Gabriel Peel Dearborn Trace Elinor Sheridan Lincoln Trace Galena Trace Douglas Trace Sarie Trace Obadiah Trace Malachi Trace Zephaniah Trace Pat Les Chris Marty Post Edwin Post Lauren Archimbault William Sharp

Lauren Trace Galena Post Elinor Trace Susan Peel Isabel Trace Isabel Trace

Droop Mud Clay War Omps Points Replete Odd Crum Pinch Muddlety

▼   ▼   ▼

Aroused all over again, sudden dream, and Sherryl Schnell somehow kneeling below attending to me. Was it indeed Sherryl? Her small curly head bobbing up and down on me going about her business, a glimpse of black eyebrows, eyelashes from above. What's got into me? Izzy would only smile. I could tell her. We can always tell each other. So it's Sherryl once again, I see, no more Mrs. Schnell.

Asleep only a few minutes? That first plunging into night, first brief dream before settling, overflow of our own good time, that's all — or some kind of wallowing in my vast idleness. But right after our imagined wedding? So quickly unfaithful, Linc.

Izzy sleeping. Sweet heart.

Wallowing idle life of bed and food and book and a little tedium hardly to be called work. Rather rearrangement, redistribution, retention. We've avoided capital, subsisted despite it — our secret pact, our tyranny. Still, a faith for them they know we believe, an opposition, a withdrawal. Others run in the chase but watch Momma and Poppa, boys — we're what you will have to compensate for. Already in childhood they set themselves to their task, their daily work, their virtue, their reproach. I at their age? Only remember down in the basement with Father, under instruction — caution, exactitude, precision, the clean barrel, the tidy bull's-eye. He was trying to interest me. And Mother so afraid.

We let our boys pass every afternoon in danger too. Do they blame me for Spode?

They all came hurtling home to tend me. They had to see it. And I was useless on some stretcher! Izzy had to hold them, watching the firemen lay out their poor smothered dog. I didn't have to see them carry away the limp fur bundle. I didn't have to see my boys' faces.

Their tears still come. Zephaniah will start and then I'll see Malachi's eyes streaming too. Obadiah will seem steady, but then he's at his desk at night, bent over, lamp out, head on arms, won't look up. They know I know now, they know I sent in the money for disposal of the body. But they'll tell it like the end of Zephaniah's story, the way we'll try to remember Spode.

But when we saw Iola walked by her Christian owners and we saw Scoper scooting down the block? Maybe they didn't like it over in Michigan the way Spode does, said Zephaniah. And Malachi didn't remind him that the story doesn't start till the coming summer. To imagine how it could all yet be prevented! Oh I miss the dog too. I loved the dog too.

"Awake, Lincoln?"

"I was thinking about our old Spode."

Her arms coming around me, humming sound, soft, stroking back of neck, long fingers circling, patting at my sudden tears, lightly brushing away . . .

▼ ▼ ▼

Have finally slept.

Today is the day we've promised them for weeks. They're already up — I can hear them running water, feet stomping about. Heavier-footed Obadiah, lengthening feet, clumsier feet. They've been excited all week. Even their Tuesday time with Mrs. Schnell went without complaints and yesterday only a half day of school, only half a week this week, and now really is spring vacation though not really spring. We're going anyway.

Isabel rolls over. There's her small face under the blanket peering out. "Have you been awake?"

"Barely."

"All night I kept waking up," she says, "and I listened to you breathe and touched your sleeping head. And you were still alive, Lincoln. You're still alive. When I saw you on the stretcher, how could I know at first? It comes back to me, that hole in the backyard, that day. And rushing away from those damn potatoes and me in one of my Troutbeck moods anyway — oh Lincoln! Do you mind I keep talking about it?"

I reach out a bare arm toward her, hiding small face, fingers touch nose and lips.

"I had them all alone, Linc," she says. "Suddenly, the boys' eyes, as if they expected to be blamed for making something so dangerous, thinking they could've lost you, buried you. If their tunnel was somehow a trap. Scared for only you, Linc, and fury in me — "

"But they believed me, Iz, I was too big around for it. They never considered I might — "

"Even so," she says, "despite that. If they felt a blame falling — "

I sit up. Is it bright beyond the window shade? A thin silvery outline.

"No, but worse, Iz, some other day, some wet afternoon late after school, and I'd hear a dull plop through the heating duct by my chair. That's all it'd be, but Spode would alert me. We'd chase down the basement stairs. Izzy, the firemen never did dig it through from the basement end. I'd never have been able to claw my way to the boys in time."

Now Isabel emerges, folds back the blanket, wide-eyed. "And I stood with them when the dog was pulled up, just all muddy fur, no shape to him anymore," she says, tears coming. "In my nightmares, Linc, they used to get swallowed up like that, and then I'd wake and tell myself they were safe upstairs and tell myself how easy we'd had it. That they never went off pedaling in traffic, weaving all over like the eggs next door. They never fought with each other, never fought with us. No one was lame or sick or slow. All locked inside at home, and our fears, our tyrannies, only a kind of unsureness of ourselves. You breathing beside me. Then I would be sure again, and feel glad, and I'd fall back asleep. It was only in my nightmares I had to taste the worry."

▼   ▼   ▼

"Lincoln, did I wake you?" says Lauren's drawling voice. "I wanted to catch you first thing. So you're going to be seeing Sarie this morning! You'll be surprised. She looks swell. All relaxed, you'll see, around the mouth and eyes. She used to be so squinted up and tight. Well, maybe it was just with me. We really needed to be apart for that time. It's a phase, right? Well, it was a phase for me too. Anyway, I think we're patching it up, but if Doug really wants the day-to-day routine, he's welcome to it. My prediction is she'll last out this term and then — switcheroo! So we'll see. Anyway, could you have her call as soon as they get there? I called at Doug's too late and I was a little reluctant to call your parents. You know? It's not been easy at all with them. But I can always talk easily to you. We should get together, you and Izzy and I. Some things I'd love to talk to you about. I mean you've been so sympathetic through all this. I never felt you'd taken sides or written me off. I've appreciated it, believe me. And even about Sarie I feel you know it wasn't just me in a selfish midlife crisis or whatever. You, Lincoln, after all, with sons, you'll be seeing soon enough how awful it gets. Fathers and sons, mothers and daughters, it's bound to be rough for a while, right? So you'll have her call me real quick? Oh and Douglas told me about your poor dog. That's so sad. Hard on the boys, I'm sure. Lord, Lincoln! Well, you take care now!"

▼   ▼   ▼

Doug's comfortable Impala glides up along the curb. The boys can hardly remember the last time Grandmother and Grandfather came out to our house. To them this is merely remarkable, no occasion for lingering resentment. Let them bounce out the front door shouting.

But really it's for Sarie — that she's come home.

Izzy and I take it more slowly down the walk, waiting our turn. Hardly does the taller thinner prettier girl have a chance to smile in our direction. They're dancing her around.

There's Mother creaking out the other side with her tan quite faded already. And frail Father from the front seat. Inside, Doug is stretching around locking all the doors.

"Unc Linc! Aunt Iz!" comes a happy voice.

When have I seen our boys so happy? They don't often allow this exuberance. So they've missed Sarie more than I knew — and the thought that she had gone upset them more.

"There's our favorite niece!" It's a strong hug she gives back. She's glad.

Hug for Izzy too, longer, tears coming. "Sometimes I was afraid I'd never see you all again" we hear Sarie saying within enfolding arms.

"Honey, honey," says Iz.

But the boys grab their cousin and dance her toward the house, so I take hold of Mother and Izzy of Father and follow slowly, Doug trailing us in his contentment now he has Sarie again.

At the front step:

"Haven't the trees grown since we were last here?" asks Mother.

"Presumably," I say.

"But it doesn't seem as mingy out here as it used to. When the buds come out you might almost get some real shade at last."

"Oh Elinor, they're perfectly respectable trees," says Father, winking toward Izzy.

Mother turns for a skeptical survey of our Greenwood, the small flat squares of late March lawn, marked off by bare uneven privet. Rodney is down the block under the hood of his rusty Mustang. It must be everybody's spring vacation.

And here comes Large Etherege, late, flipping newspapers right and left from her whirring bike.

▼　▼　▼

They've barely greeted their grandparents, taken Sarie right upstairs to impart their secrets and receive hers. Zephaniah was relieved enough when the plane brought his grandparents safely back in that icy blast of winter, but we'd only missed one of our alternating Sundays and despite their leathery skin his grandparents seemed the same ones he'd said good-bye to, fearfully, during an early thaw. But Sarie is their different cousin now. I even heard a touch of her mother's South when she spoke. She's their treasure from far away, she's seen another world, been her own self out alone in it. She's a mystery now, and maybe they don't want her to think of going away again, they want to see if they can keep her here, make sure she knows she's home.

Father's in my chair, smoothing out his pant legs. Mother moves as if this living room's too cramped for her, so few options for sitting. The low ceiling seems to press on her. She's used to an airier room poured full of dappled sunlight. Our serviceable shabby furniture, our worn carpet. And in that corner there's a golden tuft shed once by Spode. After all, it's been only a matter of weeks. A tremor in me.

"I somehow thought she wouldn't come back to us," Father's telling Izzy, who's sitting gingerly on the arm of the chair before bringing forth coffee and doughnuts. She watches him, prompting. "Well, she was one angry child," he says, "and with every good reason in the world. And she was a sad child too, wasn't she — Elinor?"

"She's still a sad child. But she's a brave child," Mother says, somewhat hoarse. "That's what happened inside her these bad months. I know. We've begun talking to each other at last."

I sit beside my mother on the couch. She's basking in a triumphant glow she feels emanating from her own pronouncement. I'm used to her methods.

"We're having such a good time, Sarie and I," she goes on. "And hasn't she become beautiful, Isabel? Cheekbones in their full glory."

"Breakfast?" says Doug, who's been investigating smells, so Izzy leads him back to the kitchen.

I'm alone with my own parents in this room. They are the same as people who have never sailed from island to green island. We looked through their photos with them and then put it all behind them. They are the same people whose granddaughter has never run away, whose son was never divorced, whose other son was never found gasping for breath in a muddy burrow.

"What's this Doug has been telling us?" Father says from our solemn quiet. "I mean about your boys at school? You didn't tell us a thing. I think we have every right to be told, Lincoln."

▼   ▼   ▼

Mother won't put her cup down. She uses it as her crystal ball, rubbing it, staring into the steaming coffee. No one else wanted a refill. Izzy has retreated with the pot.

"Mother, come on, say it," says Doug right beside her. "You said you were ready now, Mother, with Sarie home and everything changed. And this school business has done it, you said. You said!"

"Hold on, Dougie," says Father.

"What I said to Doug," Mother says, more toward Isabel, appearing behind me in the archway, "is that with two so to speak unmarried sons it seems about time to start establishing adult relations with our own grandchildren. Certainly with Sarie. We'll hold off on the Posts, they're still unfledged — but this was a warning sign, Isabel, this hint of complicity, it's too troubling about your boys. That Lincoln kept it from us is reason enough to worry. There's surely more here than we know, any of us. Isn't that the case? And you're still not looking for it. You've both been unrealistic ever since junior high school."

"Tell them!" Doug says.

"Well about money," says Mother.

"Yes, money!" Doug is poised on the cushion's edge beside her.

"Help me, Dearborn, for heaven's sake!"

Father smiles. He lets himself off easily. It's really too simple for all this fanfare. It's common sense. It's human nature. I can hear it coming. "In our comfortable way, we've lived rather simply, haven't we, your mother and I?" he says. "We've been careful, we've managed our inheritances carefully, or had them carefully managed, I should say. No blazing comets such as John Peel and his financial whiz of a son, I suppose, but steady, solid. You both have observed. And you won't take a thing from us, and we haven't tried to make you for some time. That's over. But in not too long your own children will begin constructing their own relation to the real world, and their grandmother and I have every reason to want the best for them. Sensible?"

"And especially, now," says Mother.

"They've already got it all set up for Sarie," Doug says. "She feels almost like an adult already. It's the kind of trust you show in someone that makes them leap into a whole other way of thinking about themselves. You can't deny what money means, Lincoln, to a person. I mean what money means to everyone, the poorest most of all. Think what money means to them, goddammit! They'd think you're crazier than I do!"

"Doug Doug Doug Doug," says Mother. "We're not launching another battle. We're simply announcing that there's a relationship between us and our grandchildren."

"And I might add we talked it over some with the Peels the last time we had drinks over there, which was a week ago," Father says, "and they heartily approve, of course."

"What was that you said about complicity or something, Mother?" says Isabel, fingers gripping my shoulder a bit fiercely.

"Don't all families fight about money?" Doug says to me. "But ours is the only one approaching it this way, you can be damn sure."

"Mother, if you're imagining we have three delinquents in the making — "

A torrent of footsteps from above. Soon they're with us. Are we going to keep talking now?

"Sarie, come talk to us," I say. "We've hardly seen you yet."

"No, but first, Poppa, we have to show her in the basement," says Obadiah. "You know, where you almost got buried alive."

"Don't remind me, child," his grandmother says.

"Spode wasn't there then," says Zephaniah before anyone else says anything.

"Come on, really, is this how you're letting them handle it, Lincoln!" says Doug, exasperation in his bugged-out eyes.

"Really he's over in Michigan," says Zephaniah, but Sarie has put her arms around him from behind.

"Zephaniah," she says, "but show me anyway, the place, you know," and she catches Malachi's eye.

"You kids come right back up," Doug says. "There's doughnuts and juice. And we want to talk to you! Talk, as in conversation. Like a normal family. Hear me?"

Slam of basement door.

"But you know what Galena thinks, of course," he goes on. "You can imagine her on the subject. It's not really money, not as long as you have a roof over your head. Money's one of those things we use, I mean to talk about something else. That's her line. Too much shrink!"

"I keep thinking how it's Galena who really wanted to take off on a spring drive, Lincoln, and just drive and drive," says Mother. "She gets everyone else taking off but herself. Ed gets what he wants, doesn't he — the classic only child. Well, I have to hand it to him. Aren't you going to at least stop in on the Fox River?"

"Maybe on our way back," Izzy says.

"But I was saying," says Doug. He's holding a third doughnut before his lips as if to decide whether to save Sarie from temptation.

Mother turns. Doug always sat beside her in childhood. His same body, reduced to quarter size, whiskers retracted, hairline lowered, in little boy's clothes, a whine in his voice, but eyes as sorrowful, as wide — there he still is.

"But Galena's line," he says, "is that it all has to do with control. You know what control has to do with? I mean what it all goes back to? I mean the function we all have to learn to control? How's that grab you, Pop?"

"It's not to be entirely discounted," says Father.

Scraping noises below rising through the vent.

"But it's money we're talking about," says Mother, "and it doesn't matter what it means, Douglas, because it's going to be dispensed from one party to another, and third parties really have nothing to say and that's that. There seem to be certain tax advantages anyway in skipping generations. As if they somehow knew, the powers that be, that alliances do finally get forged and the common enemy finally is faced. Time is with us, age is with us, my dears."

Father chuckles. "Your mother's a droll woman," he tells me. "But Lincoln, really, this is nothing so drastic. It simply seems to us, doesn't it, Elinor, that if your boys were to be told, now, quite straightforwardly, what their financial status is to be in a mere decade, if not, heaven forfend, sooner, then they might take the longer view more confidently. The little friends they make might have less influence on them. Is that unreasonable?"

Such giggles from the basement below. What goes on?

Zephaniah, who hadn't dared go down there again till now, his silly laugh too.

"Their little friends?" says Izzy. She is being polite. She stands behind me, patient, knowing we have only to make it through this morning and then we're off.

"Look," says Doug, "I'm their uncle. They were my mainstays when Sarie was gone. I love those kids. I'm looking out for them too. You really are cranks, like Gale says. I mean look at that bookshelf. I was just noticing. All those moldy old books. Shelves of famous authors' worst books. You're the only people I know who religiously avoid the finer things. Who bothers to read A Son at the Front or Mantrap? Yesteryear's remainders! What's with you, Izzy? Haven't you ever heard of The House of Mirth or Main Street? And look at that stack of Linc's atlases. Try finding one since World War Two! Sometimes I want to kidnap those boys out of here!"

More giggles. They're listening, all four of them, listening to us grown-ups, from vent to vent. They could be all over the house, whisperings and giggles, rising through the walls, emerging under beds, behind doors. The house alive with them.

▼   ▼   ▼

"Douglas tells me you've become quite a reader, Sarie." She's drying while I wash.

"Unc Linc, you don't ever read mysteries, do you?"

"I thought it was dragon trilogies."

"Well, I went through most of those. They got sort of boring. I mean they just go on and on. But see, mysteries aren't ever that long and you know who's going to be in it and it's like it's a puzzle and the answer's already in there. My aunt Lindy had some. My other aunt Louisa tried to get me reading William Faulkner. Forget it! They made us read The Bear back in school. That was the last straw. I was out of there! Unc Linc, where do these go?"

I point to the shelf for saucers and the hooks for cups, our best china, nothing souvenir about it. "Grandmother's a mystery fiend," I tell her.

"Yeah, we've been talking. You know, no one's been mad at me. Not even Mom. That's a funny thing. I was so mad when I left, Unc Linc. I stayed so mad so long. And then I just wasn't so mad. And I sort of got myself more together. Darrell Quong and all that mess — I don't even believe it ever happened. The thing about being my generation is you really survive. I mean mostly. And when you survive for a while you decide it's not all bad, there's good things too. You know, my dad, he's been good, he's been really good. I didn't see that about him before."

"He'd still like to kill his older brother occasionally."

"Oh Unc Linc! They showed me! Where you could've been killed. Really, you could've! They were showing me where it fell in on Spode. It's solid mud down in there! Then Zephaniah started in crying so I got going on more funny stories about my crazy cousins down South."

She's standing in the morning light with the dish towel. Beyond glass, everyone else out in the backyard. I'll be pulling up this putty soon, setting ahead clocks. Out there the widow's poodle's yipping at them from behind the mud heap Izzy's sculpted into a shapely mound. Out there Izzy's beautiful. Can't tell from her soft eyes how cautiously we look at each other these weeks. Under us something's shifted. How we've even let Mrs. Schnell see the boys on Tuesdays. Are we afraid? It's harder for Izzy than me because she still wants to be my faith. Oh I want to be hers too. But haven't told her why I trespassed or Obadiah's secrets that I read. Notebook unretrieved, lost history. Why I trespassed?

Out there she's explaining to Mother about the rock garden. Mother's doubtful eye, and Father awkward with the boys, attempting a head pat, then his gaze upwards, interested in patterns of bare branches. And Doug skulking along the property line. His new life's begun too. There's one thing I might just ask my niece here, folding the dish towel.

"Did they tell you what they thought I was doing, Sarie, down there in the tunnel? Do they blame me for the dog at all? Or being where I shouldn't have been? You can tell me. It's hard to figure out what your kids are really thinking."

Not sure of me. Could we become new allies? "Well, Malachi was explaining how you went down there to double-check on their job, you know, to make sure it was safe for them, with the earth packed, you know, solid enough and not going to cave in on them. He said how you always check on them, just to be sure, not to bother them or anything, but making sure they're all right, you know? That's what fathers are for, Obadiah said. I told him didn't I know! Like my dad wanting to drive down and bring me home. And I wasn't even going to let him. Unc Linc, you know, I'm glad you all waited around this morning so I could see everybody. I couldn't have waited one more week, really I couldn't't."

I can only hug her again. Close against her ear, but I can't tell her of my terrible lacks.

▼　▼　▼

We have crossed the Fox where it divides East Dundee from West, and on we've driven. They've never been so far from home. Even beyond the Dundees there still lingered an aura of the city for some miles, and then how it all opened up and we began to see an older world of fields and barns and clumps of black oaks against the sky. And the land begins to roll and there's a sense of gradual ascension onto the swelling continent. Did it scare them? And through Stillman Valley, stopping at the monument, and to the Rock River, crossing it once, and at Oregon back again to picnic at Black Hawk's feet. It was suddenly my own old days. I was there again, with my own family. The huge Indian rose behind us and our fast-food take-out Styrofoam containers, and the boys, cautious, looked across the river to where the land swelled still more, like a wave, faintest haze of green bud on tree, distant gold of last year's harvest stubble in field.

So we've followed Black Hawk's westward gaze.

"I didn't know the Falcon could go so far," said Zephaniah. "We went a hundred miles already." They've all been leaning over the back of the front seat, watching Izzy trace our voyage on the map. Mount Morris. Lanark. Savanna.

And then the largest river, into which, farther down, all the rain on my parents' backyard finally somehow finds its way. Marne, Fox, Rock. Father of Waters. We sat on grass, drank the pop they got from the last gas station's cold drink machine. And I think the boys were getting used to being somewhere new to them. Malachi stopped fidgeting. Obadiah took his windbreaker off and lay back on it — it was just warm enough in the sun. Zephaniah leaning on Izzy's knees. "That's Iowa over there. You've never seen another state before." This educating decision of ours, this cautious attempt.

Then driving along the Palisades and up into higher country, toward the town my sister's named for, where we'll spend our night. The Falcon isn't used to such elevations. With all five of us and suitcases, it moogles and cleeps excessively. But now we're cresting, the high road, the rolling budding country, gnarled black walnut trees in twisted gulches and cows already out cropping first spring grass in the far lower meadows. Soon in May, when the wind's brush makes all the green leaves and grasses quiver —

"Look," says Obadiah, long arm straining over and across Izzy's lap. "One thousand two hundred and forty-one feet above sea level. Charles Mound. We never were so high up, were we, Momma? We never could see this far."

The land rich, the farms poor, I'm thinking. Strange old world of mine, last seen, me in backseat then, some thirty years long gone. Father telling us about the history of lead mining and old Ulysses retiring to Galena after the war and Father preparing us to understand the things we'd see, to see into them. Preparing us.

Izzy musing too, something of her silent own.

"You know, Poppa," says Obadiah. He must feel like talking. Something's astir in him. "Grandfather asked me, out in the backyard when Momma was telling her garden idea, he asked me about school, I mean about what happened. He wanted to hear about us and Mrs. Schnell and what it's like when we go talk to her. But the funny thing, Poppa, does Grandfather know Mrs. Schnell actually?"

"Of course not," I say.

"But see, he knew that we told her how he could pay for those computers. I mean we didn't really mean he should but we were telling her once how our grandfather could pay if it was us that did it. And Gramp too, both of them together, they could afford it, couldn't they, because they're rich. And see, Ivo and his brother, they couldn't pay, and Brad lives with only his mom. But how did Grandfather even know we told Mrs. Schnell that?"

"Tell me again," I say. "Grandfather asked you in the yard if you told Mrs. Schnell he'd pay for the computers?"

"No no no," says Obadiah, his chin sharp on my right shoulder. "Poppa, Mrs. Schnell didn't go ask him to pay or anything. Grandfather knows we didn't actually do vandalism. We just had some scary ideas we were talking about and then Pribyl and Tokarsky told us we were dicks."

Zephaniah gets the giggles, so Malachi tries shutting him up.

"No funny business in the backseat!" Izzy proclaims.

"But Momma, Poppa," says Obadiah, "see, I think Mrs. Schnell went and told Grandfather. You know, to find out more about it. I mean we go in there on Tuesdays and talk with her about any old thing she wants. We don't mind her so much now. Brad and them aren't in school anymore even. They're in trouble for good. Mrs. Schnell thinks it's peculiar we don't hate them like the other kids do. All the kids at school really hate Brad and Shaun and Ivo. Even though Miss Carswell said they had to try to forgive, but all the kids hate them anyway for doing that to our school. Mrs. Schnell keeps trying to see if we hate them a little too. She says doesn't it make us mad what they did? We all say no."

"I tell her it wasn't a good idea though," says Zephaniah.

"We all tell her it wasn't a good idea," Obadiah says, and Malachi leans forward and nods too. They're squeezed in between our heads. I can't see out the rearview mirror on this winding road. "But she said our grandfather might have something to say about what he could afford or not. So that's what Grandfather said to me in the yard. You know, Obadiah, he said, there's some precious things, he said, that he wants to spend his money on. That's what he's been saving it up for. And not on some bunch of broken machines. And not on somebody else's kids' mistakes. That's what he said exactly, Poppa. But how did he know we thought he could pay?"

▼   ▼   ▼

The boys have gone up ahead of us, in a rush, then more careful from the first landing on. They've never climbed an open wooden stairway in the wind. They don't know how high up it will suddenly feel on this height of land. But Izzy and I are being careful only because we'll need our breath. We know these towers don't tumble down, people don't blow off them.

"Looks like we'll have to shut some mouths when we get back home," she says, stepping slowly beside me.

"Iz, it keeps coming to me, I keep hearing Mother saying how time is with them, age is with them. Did you hear her? It was almost her threat."

"Oh crap! But they're all in cahoots — Schnell, Traces, Peels, Posts. Unholy alliances — haven't we detected them everywhere, Lincoln, one form or another, going way back? When we were kids nothing ever looked quite right to us. We're still entrenched! It hasn't changed. We've been holding out a long time. Why shouldn't time be with us not them? Is their world any better?" My dogmatist.

Huff puff I go at the first landing.

She's stopped with me to look across the wide land, arms on each other's shoulders. Have we seen anything as beautiful in our lives together?

"But still — " I try to say.

"Lincoln?"

"But with the boys now — Iz, what I'm afraid of — well, this recapitulation we've managed to engender, in them, it won't be stopping at eleven — and what if somehow we've started ourselves again too? So again we'll meet each other, Iz. We'll fall in love again and want to spend all our hours together. But what I'm afraid of now — if it isn't as sure as it was, if it's more dangerous, if we start discovering, along with them, oh what? Unfaithfulness? Fury? Despair? More afraid for us than them — "

"For us, Linc?"

"Poppa!" "Momma!" "Poppa, Momma!" from above.

▼   ▼   ▼

Blue sky, gray cloud, a declining sun, earth — and earth for miles. Wooden platform, people's initials all over it, a raft floating up in this crisp blueness. Our boys, wind lifting their brown hair.

"What's all this wind?" asks Malachi. It was calmer down there by the small-seeming car.

"This particular wind, I think," says Izzy, stretching out her ten bare fingers to test it, "is blowing us spring."